The Wound

FRENCH VOICES

FRENCH
VOICES

Winner of the French Voices Award
www.frenchbooknews.com

THE
WOUND

LAURENT MAUVIGNIER

Translated by DAVID BALL *and* NICOLE BALL
Foreword by NICK FLYNN

University of Nebraska Press
Lincoln and London

French Voices logo designed by Serge Bloch.

This work, published as part of a program
providing publication assistance, received
financial support from the French Ministry
of Foreign Affairs, the Cultural Services of
the French Embassy in the United States, and
FACE (French American Cultural Exchange).

Library of Congress Cataloging-
in-Publication Data
Mauvignier, Laurent.
[Hommes. English]
The wound / Laurent Mauvignier;
translated by David Ball and Nicole Ball;
foreword by Nick Flynn.
pages   cm. — (French voices)
"Originally published in French as
Des Hommes? 2009 Les Editions
de Minuit"—Title page verso.
Includes bibliographical references and index.
ISBN 978-0-8032-3987-6 (paperback: alk. paper)
ISBN 978-0-8032-7653-6 (epub)
ISBN 978-0-8032-7654-3 (mobi)
ISBN 978-0-8032-7655-0 (pdf)
I. Ball, David, translator. II. Ball,
Nicole, translator. III. Title.
PQ2673.A836D4713 2015
843'.914 — dc23
2014039726

Set in Galliard by Renni Johnson.
Designed by N. Putens.

And your wound, where is your wound?

I wonder where that wound is nestled, where it is hidden, the secret wound where every man runs to take shelter if his pride is violated, when it is wounded. That wound— which has become his inner self—is what he will inflate and fill. Every man knows how to find it and inhabit it so completely that he becomes the wound itself, a kind of secret, aching heart.

JEAN GENET, *The Tightrope Walker*

FOREWORD
Nick Flynn

Afternoon. Evening. Night. Morning.

The Wound is a quiet novel with a war in the middle of it. We begin in a small French village on one semi-eventful day, a day when something that has been lurking below the surface of every other day—a tension from all that has been left unspoken—rises up for a moment in the form of a few wounding words and a thoughtless (sinister? premeditated?) act. Once that dark thread is plucked it leads us back to all we have tried to forget, all we have tried to leave behind. I say "we" because this is a novel that very quickly pulls us into its orbit. The narrator walks us through this incident and its aftermath and then rewinds the frames to when the protagonist, Bernard, was a young man in a war. Bernard came home from that war and he has become an outcast—unable to turn away from what had happened, or perhaps the pressure of turning away has distorted him. The narrator lived through that war as well, along with his cousin Bernard; he carries some photographs of those days, photographs which keep changing in meaning the more he looks at them. *The Wound* ends up being about time and the masks we all wear and how blood runs in both directions at once, both away and toward whatever wounds we try to ignore. The tension builds slowly, surely—it takes its time, yet each word, each gesture, is utterly gripping. Within a few pages you know you are in the realm of something magnificent.

Afternoon. Evening. Night. Morning—this is how Laurent Mauvignier divides the book, these are the names he gives each section. The story unfolds in one day, until we land in Night, which travels, as nights do, through time and space, bringing us closer to the unknown, the mysterious, the out-of-sight, the dreamworld.

In *Achilles in Vietnam*, Jonathan Shay's study of war and its aftermath, the author proposes that the Greeks wrote their plays, in part, to try to understand the soldiers coming home after their endless wars; what soldiers bring back inside them, and what they don't—or can't—talk about. Why Ajax slaughters all the cattle in that tent, say. *The Wound* begins in the same silence, after the incident that is, in retrospect, both predictable and unfathomable. A small cruelty that leads back in time to a larger one, the one no one wants to talk about.

The books that come closest to *The Wound*'s energies are J. M. Coetzee's *Waiting for the Barbarians* and Albert Camus's *The Stranger*. Like those masterpieces, *The Wound* has the feel and texture of inevitability, as if every word had been floating along the surface of some hidden river below the earth's crust all this time. Until this moment no one had yet found the crack, no one had simply bent down, reached through it, touched the water. *The Wound* is contained in a day, and what happens on that day—perhaps on any day, if we could only touch it—reveals the entirety of the universe. Something happens, and through it we try to understand all that has happened.

At the end of *The Wound* is a glossary; turn to it now. Find the words and places that may or may not help in reading the book (*wadi, harkis, bicot*). Many of the words are from the Arabic, others are places of battle or massacre (*Verdun, Oradour-sur-Glane*). Scattered throughout the book are references to a handful of images that get returned to over and over—photographs, masks, stones . . . each one takes on talismanic significance by the end. In the end it is, perhaps, simply about wrestling with what it means to tell a story as the narrator describes it:

> Maybe none of that matters, that whole story doesn't matter, maybe you don't know what a real story is if you haven't lifted the ones underneath, the only ones that count, they're like ghosts, our ghosts, that accumulate and are like the stones of a strange house where you lock yourself in all alone, each one of us in his own house, and with what windows, how many windows? And at that moment, I thought we should move as little as possible during our lifetime so as not to generate the past, as we do, every day, the past that creates stones, and the stones, walls. And now we're here watching ourselves grow old, not understanding why Bernard is out there in that shack, with his dogs so old now, and his memory so old, and his hatred so old too that all the words we could say can't do very much.

The narrator is in a car, an echo of someone else trapped in a car in one great novels of the twentieth century—the eponymous *Mrs. Bridge*, trapped in her car, watching the snow fall. And here we are in the twenty-first century, holding a book that looks back into the twentieth, to a central event in the history of France, which leads to Algeria and its war for independence and sets the stage for our future "modern" warfare of neighborhood street battles, an enemy who looks just like the people the occupiers are trying to protect (or subjugate—it depends upon your vantage point), and the introduction of torture as a means to cow a population. The pattern was set in Algeria and it has been repeated in Vietnam, in El Salvador, Iraq, the Congo, the list goes on and on, with predictably disastrous results. *The Wound* brings us closer into the mind of those for whom the war never really ends, and how they—we—carry these wounds with us into our homes. All of this takes place during Night, as if it were all a dream—or a long nightmare—we had yet to escape, because until now we hadn't found the words.

The Wound

AFTERNOON

IT WAS PAST A QUARTER TO ONE AND HE WAS SURPRISED everyone wasn't staring at him, surprised no one showed astonishment because he, too, had made an effort, he was wearing a matching jacket and pants, a white shirt, and one of those imitation leather ties like they used to make twenty years ago and you can still find in discount stores.

Today, people will say he didn't smell too bad. They won't make sarcastic comments about him coming for a free meal and for once he won't have to pretend he dropped by at the spur of the moment. They'll call him Woodsmoke as they have for years, and some will remember he has a real name under the filth and the smell of wine and the neglect of his sixty-three-year-old body.

They'll remember that behind Woodsmoke there used to be Bernard. They'll hear his sister call him by his first name: Bernard. They'll remember that he hasn't always been a sponger who lives off others. They'll watch him on the sly so as not to put him on his guard. They'll still see him with the same yellow-gray hair from tobacco smoke and charcoal fire, the same bushy, dirty mustache. And those blackheads on his pockmarked, bulbous nose, round as an apple. And the blue eyes, with the skin pink and swollen under the lids. The broad, solid body. And this time, if you paid attention, you would see the traces of a comb on his swept-back hair; you would see he made an effort at cleanliness. And you could even tell yourself he wasn't drunk and didn't look too nasty.

People had seen him park his moped in front of Patou's like he did every day, and then go in there for a bit before crossing the street to come in here, into the community center, to be with his sister Solange, who was celebrating her sixtieth birthday and her retirement with all of us—cousins, brothers, friends.

And it's not exactly then, but afterward, of course, when it was all over and we had left that Saturday behind, and the empty hall with its smell of cold tobacco and wine, its ripped, soiled paper tablecloths—and outside, the snow on the concrete slab in front of the entrance had finished covering up the footprints of all those guests who had gone home to wonder over the events of the day—it was only then that I, too, would see every scene again, astonished to find each of them so clear in my memory, so present.

I will remember that when people started giving their gifts I had looked at him, Woodsmoke, standing slightly apart from everybody, fiddling with something in the pocket of his jacket. Actually, that jacket—I'd never seen him with that jacket, but I knew it. I mean, I'd never seen it on him, a suede jacket with a woolen lining on the collar. It looked old, and I had the time to think it had belonged to one of their brothers, his and Solange's brothers, who must have given him some old things in exchange for a little help, a cord of wood to move into the garage, or even for nothing, just to give his brother some clothes he didn't want anymore.

I said that to myself as I was looking at him because he still had his right hand in his pocket and that hand seemed to be holding or manipulating something, a pack of cigarettes, maybe, but no, of course not, I'd seen him take out his pack of cigarettes and put it into his back pocket.

People had begun to talk louder and laugh, too — a laugh that billowed from one mouth to another as corks of *mousseux* popped and glasses clinked together. Dozens and dozens of Solange's friends had filed by, acquaintances, faces as familiar as the ones in the photos she kept behind glass in her living room cabinet.

Come on, Solange, you have to drink.

And Solange drank.

Come on, Solange.

And Solange had smiled, talked, laughed in her turn, and then we had almost forgotten she was there as she went from one group to another, for groups had formed according to affinities and relationships, some slipping from one group to another and others, on the contrary, avoiding them altogether.

I don't know if she avoided going up to him, knowing she couldn't get out of that invitation, because I know how much she dreaded it even more than she dreaded the presence of the Owl and her husband, and the presence of Jean-Jacques, Micheline, and Evelyne and a few others, too. But his presence. His. Woodsmoke. Bernard. It wasn't the first time I'd had the feeling she was uncomfortable because of the guilt she felt when she would hide out in her kitchen so as not to open the door to him; when he'd go down to La Bassée, and after a prolonged stop at Patou's would show up in front of her gate yelling he loved his sister, he wanted to see his sister, she had to talk to him, she had to, she had to, he would say, howling so loud he became threatening sometimes because nobody would come and all the new houses around would only echo back silence and emptiness. Silence and houses hollow as caves in which his voice seemed to

5

get lost, dwindle, and fade away until he finally gave up, grumbling all the way down the road to his moped. Which would take him back home or else back to Patou's, where he'd probably end up drowning his disappointment in another drink, the last one, for the road, until he'd let Patou convince him that Solange had to work, people have to work, you know, a single woman with kids.

And he would end up saying yeah, sure, I understand, my sister who's all alone, my sister and her kids. He would lower his eyes and blush at all the unfairness, at that whole mess, he'd say to the customers, whoever was willing to hear, or rather to the ones who had nothing better to do than hear him—rather than listen to him—despite Jean-Marc's voice lecturing him nicely, or Patou's,

Yes, Woodsmoke, we know, yes, Woodsmoke, your sister, yes, that's right, Woodsmoke.

And on his way out he'd always end up spitting near the door, always in the same spot, always staggering, near collapse but never collapsing, standing solid even in that way he had of being pathetic, weak, and dying all the way into his heart.

But there was his impatience. His way of smiling. A kind of hostility in his presence, or distrust, already, like always, or even, yes, a kind of condescension.

That's what I've always told myself.

Even when I saw him like that, scrubbed rather than clean, when all his cleanliness suggested the strain, the work, the determination he had put into making himself presentable.

And that afternoon I watched him for a long time. I don't know why, but my eyes kept coming back to him. He wasn't aware of me. I would watch him as he exchanged a few words with Jean-Marcel, with Francis, watch him smile at the children he didn't recognize.

6

And then suddenly he made up his mind.

I saw him straighten up, tense up and look around frankly, not surreptitiously as he had up to now, but with his neck stretched and his eyes wide open. I had the time to see him take something out of his pocket, but something too little for me to see, or understand. A black shape I hardly saw before it was swallowed up by the palm of his hand. His fingers closed immediately. Fist clenched, wide, thick and rough.

And then he walked forward. And then he called Solange. And then, as he kept walking toward her, he called Solange louder and louder. Until people stopped to look at him for a moment, surprised at his burst of energy, at this movement, suddenly, at his smile and energy; I would have said it was actually the faith of a visionary (but I have my reasons for thinking that, seeing it like that), but that wasn't it, it was the joy of a man who was a little strange and out of it, who probably didn't like being there, who certainly wouldn't have come if Solange hadn't specifically invited him. I mean, he wouldn't have come if one of his brothers or another sister had invited him—not one of them. He spoke to them from time to time and even accepted a few rare invitations sometimes, but only to thank them for a handout—old clothes—or out of the need to eat, out of hunger, because hunger drove him out of his house.

They got out of his way to let him go by. It took awhile for the surprise to swell, for all the movements, the looks and the comments to stop. It took some time for all the movements to slow down and stabilize. It took something more than a gesture or a laugh, it took a scream.

Not a scream of horror, nor terror. No. A voice breaking from stupefaction, a surge of energy and something shattering against him. It was only slightly above the voices and the attention that was vaguely floating in his general direction, toward his voice and movements, and his gesture toward Solange, but it wasn't insistent enough for them to be quiet, for everybody to listen.

Yet someone sees, always.

And here it's Marie-Jeanne who was the first to see, because she was near Solange and at the moment he came over to the table Solange was sort of leaning on—her hand resting on the edge of the tray, flat on the paper tablecloth—Marie-Jeanne was trying to taste another one of those marvelous petits fours shaped like a little tart with anchovies or cream of tuna when she must have moved, turned around, whatever, and seen him in front of her, suddenly, right there now, his outstretched hand holding that little box (not black, as I had thought at first, but a very deep blue encircled by gold edging) for her, to give her this present she was not expecting and saw coming out of his big callused hand—that man who was so improbably here, in front of her, so fearsome that she would have cried out anyway, even if he had nothing in his hand, even if he hadn't held out his hand or his fist, or that little deep blue box.

So yes, you have to hear that particular cottony silence, and the snow that had started to fall again, perhaps, the silence of snowy days, as if something of that silence had entered the hall. You could also have said it was an awkward moment, but the moment was so short, so fleeting. Because Marie-Jeanne got ahold of herself right away, straightened up, stuffed down a petit four and then laughed,

Oh, you frightened me!

Without his moving or saying anything, because she had already started to giggle again,

You want to propose to me?

And everybody started to laugh, well, not everybody yet, no, only the people who were right next to them and had witnessed the scene and could testify later, after he left, that everything was definitively settled and over at that very moment. Because he didn't laugh at all. He looked at Marie-Jeanne, her iridescent pearl necklace glittering on her large, bulging bust, her apple-green dress and her hooded collar, her dyed hair with glints of mauve and mouse gray, and her smiling mouth, laughing now that he was the one feeling astonishment and stupor, not her anymore. And him not stammering, not a word from him as he faced her, while she was laughing and looking around for the approval of the others, for the approval of her husband, Jean-Claude, who had walked over when he heard his wife and then kept laughing, him, the husband, wanting to be cute, thinking he was funny, suddenly drawing himself up, blustering almost as he repeated,

Watch out, I've got my eye on you, pal.

With other voices coming in behind his,

Hey, Woodsmoke, how about a little tact!

That Woodsmoke, what a playboy!

Watch out, I've got my eye on you, pal.

And he wasn't laughing at all as he looked at Jean-Claude, listening to the laughs and then coming back toward Marie-Jeanne, whose nervous laughter was sprinkling crumbs of tuna tartlet onto the apple green of her dress.

With a sharp but discreet movement he shut his mouth and perhaps even bit his lip under his big, grayish yellow mustache. But that's not certain. Not sure. Because his face was like a red, puffy mask pierced by two liquid blue eyes veiled with gray the color of rainwater; and that veil wasn't tears, that veil was nothing, Woodsmoke was nothing but a block of silence that had retracted, closing his hand over the deep blue box.

Solange came over.

Actually, I'm wrong, she only turned toward him. Yes, that's it. She was standing next to him. Because she was right next to him. She just made a move to turn around. To pick up her hand, take her hand off the tablecloth. To turn around. Then her brother was suddenly in front of her.

She let a moment go by before she said anything. Because at first she didn't understand that he'd come toward her to hold out the package he hadn't given at the same time as the others. As if he, of course, naturally, didn't have to do what other people did. He wouldn't have to mix with the others. But maybe I'm giving him motives he never had. Because it wasn't his scorn, his haughtiness, his air of a ruined, disillusioned aristocrat. Maybe he only wanted to give it to his sister in a more intimate, less solemn way than under the judgmental eyes of all the guests. Because he must have thought and believed—and he was right—that the guests would judge his gift more severely than any other, because of that question, right, which did pop up in the minds of a few of them at first and then all of them: you really wonder what a guy who doesn't have a thing can possibly give.

They didn't have to wait long.

Happy birthday, he said. And the left hand moved toward Solange's hand, the thick, dry, pink fingers, puffy but also wounded, worn by the cold and the jobs he always did without gloves, suddenly grabbing Solange's hand and bringing it toward his own, his other hand. Like he thought no one would see.

And this time he wished her happy birthday again, but smiling, his voice so weak and shaky that no one really heard it, they only sensed it under the voices talking further off, the voices of children shouting as they played and ran, and the cackling of the three old women sitting over there on gray plastic chairs, shivering near the heater. Then that silence and astonishment when Solange lowered her eyes to the box, recognizable by its format but also because you could read on it, in golden letters, the name of the Buchet family, jewelers-watchmakers for two generations.

She looked at her brother without daring to open the box. She let her incredulity take over her face, spread over every one of her features, and leave its imprint for a long time, very deeply. And sometimes she would start to smile (it was almost a laugh, even, when she turned her eyes toward the others, to the ones who were right next to her, or, on the contrary, a bit further away, like me, behind a group of a few people who had stopped moving and talking, and had suddenly forgotten the cigarette they were holding, like the glass in their hands).

Okay, open it, Solange.

I think that was the moment she figured out everything that must have happened for it to come to this, at the precise moment she held a jewel box in her hand—because, clearly, it was a piece of jewelry—which she didn't dare open because she knew, not what was in it but the consequences, the doubts, the risks, and already, I'm sure, the fear, it was enough to hear and watch how the silence was both porous and thick, how it went through the smoke and breath of the guests in the hall.

And him, the only thing on his mind must have been whether she was going to like his present. And his heart must have been pounding, beating like mad at this question, only at this question, when all around him people were already beginning to wonder, exasperated by the wait, telling themselves, wondering, I'm dreaming, a piece of jewelry, a jewel, he couldn't give a jewel, how could he give a jewel, she has to open the box and look, she doesn't want to because she knows, yes, she knows what she will find on the blue velvet lining, she knows she'll have to silence her fear and the question everyone will have in mind but him, just him, whose only question will no longer mean anything,

Do you like it?

Do you like it?

The question already on the edge of his lips, stirring in his mouth, ready to come out in the form of a whisper, a prayer, but for now only an intense wait, his eyes fixedly staring into hers, where he would soon have nothing to see but terror and incomprehension. Yet she hesitated. She did everything to put off the moment. To retreat. To not. Not open. Not look into the box, just smile at him and smile around her. She closed her eyes then opened them. She began breathing again. She tentatively uttered a few shreds of phrases, of embarrassed thanks not addressed to him, her brother, but to everybody. Since everybody was waiting for her to speak, to put an end to her smile already and stop saying empty phrases that didn't mean anything.

You shouldn't have, Bernard. I, I don't get it.

And her face going pale, her skin white under the makeup and soon livid, as if blood, life, ideas, and any possibility of holding out while facing him were deserting her, were evaporating or burying themselves in the folds of her body.

So open it, Solange.

Yes. Yes, yes, of course. Yes, sure I'll open it, I have to, am I dumb. That Bernard. He's so crazy. He's crazy, right? Really. I. I.

And that moment of panic in her eyes when she opened the box and the brooch appeared.

A big brooch of shimmering gold. Polished gold with diamonds in it, enhanced by a flower motif in mother-of-pearl.

I hesitated over a beetle I really liked, he said, as if to defend himself already or explain the choice he had made. Since you like brooches, I thought you'd like this one, he said.

She replied with a nod, in a kind of rush, with something close to terror in the movements of her features.

And you could see that her eyes were looking around her for some kind of help, for a solution, some energy or the strength to answer, but around her the same question showed on every face.

How could he have done that?

How is it possible, with what money?

A guy with no money who sponges off other people, off all the others around him, their eyes going from the brooch to him and from him to the brooch, then from the brooch to them, then from one to the other, eyes asking the same questions, already revealing the same stupefaction and, already, anger.

Solange remained silent, she was moved, too, not just petrified or shocked or troubled but perhaps mostly moved, I think, that's what I think anyway, but at that moment I thought she felt fear, an indecisive fear, blurry and vague, related to what would soon happen rather than to that moment, the present moment, holding and looking at the little blue box in her hand from which she did not dare take the brooch.

So take it, Solange. Put it on.

Yes yes, of course.

I had just walked over and I was now at his side, right next to him. I could smell that odor, a mixture of soap, of cleanliness so raw it must have scraped off the scales on his skin and the skin with them. And that indefinable odor of dirty people, that persistence of dirtiness, bitter and sour, that lingering, sweetish smell of urine.

And I saw Solange's fingers trembling when they grasped the brooch. She turned around to put the box down on the tablecloth. She took off her laurel-shaped brooch, then looked at the brooch again. A long time. Then alternately looking at her brother. Then around her, first bursting into a silly laugh, giggling almost to hide to herself that she was blushing, strangling too, a little, strangling the words and the stupor they were concealing. She pinned the brooch to the spot where the other one had been. She remained like that, let me give you a kiss, then she held out her face to her brother, and they kissed.

So you do like it. You like it?

Yes, of course I like it.

Solange answered in a halting voice, her delivery more and more false, lacking conviction, as if what she cared about was above all to get this over with as fast as possible, for everyone to go home, for Woodsmoke to leave, for him not to have come at all so she wouldn't have to live through this moment, through the lie, through that *of course* which she did not believe, she no more than anybody else believed it, with all of us standing around her as if we were gathered together around a fire not for the heat and light, just drawn by the crackling of a scene, a story to tell, the anecdote of the guy who's broke and gives his sister, right before the eyes of everybody who'd once given him a handout, a brooch that none of them would ever have the means to give anybody.

And Solange's eyes looking around for help that didn't come, as all of them suddenly discovered in their hands a cigarette to light or put out, a half-empty glass to fill right away or the other way around, to empty very quickly, in one gulp.

Because Solange went on for a little while. Tears not suffocating her yet, just a terrible, monstrous embarrassment swelling up in her throat, and now incomprehension in her eyes. And he, he had begin to laugh, yes, laugh at first, both hands sliding into his pockets and then one hand coming out to stroke his mustache as if to comb it, flatten it against his mouth before the same hand dove into his back pocket and came up with a pack of Gitanes. And that shy air he had when he answered his sister before she could even speak,

Don't worry about that.

Bernard. It costs a fortune.

Don't worry about it I said.

How did you pay?

You like it?

That's not the point.

So what is the point?

And suddenly, something like . . . emotion. A rush that knotted up her belly. And against which she was throwing all her strength. Her voice got hoarse and she started laughing a little too shrilly, a bit pathetically it seemed to me. Actually, it wasn't only that her laugh was pathetic, it was also theatrical, since she was well aware that everybody was already beginning to wonder and make comments, for the moment only with glances, little shifts of voices and elbows, a hand placed on an arm, a mouth in a doubtful, circumspect pout, a head nodding meaningfully, looks, gestures and signs, raised eyebrows, knit brows, and expressions lingering long enough to be noticed.

Nicole looked at me and I had the time to realize she wanted to intervene, without really knowing how, any more than I did.

And that went on for a while.

The Owl with her coat buttoned up to the chin, its blond sable fur dusty and dull, came charging over, not to ask for explanations, not yet, not her and not Evelyne—at that point the first to come over and take a close look—one of the sisters, Evelyne along with a sister-in-law, the wife of Jean-Jacques (he probably didn't care at all, out there near the kitchen talking with Pingeot and Chefraoui. Both of them walked over. Then Marie-Jeanne. Solange looked at me from a distance. I walked over, too. Nicole, on the contrary, stepped back.

I stayed there, letting my eyes linger on the backs of the people I now saw walking forward, coming over to Solange without really daring to speak yet, or stammering out what must have already been burning their lips. And soon it would be the same for the others, the ones who drew near, who were there, so near, so interested, the brothers and sisters, the brother-in-laws and sister-in-laws—but not the friends, not the acquaintances, not the others, the ones passing through, whose presence was not the most expected—and I saw how Solange hesitated to raise her hands to the brooch, then openly decided to take it off, giving some pretext or other, I don't know, maybe nothing, it doesn't go with my sweater, it's too gorgeous, yes, too gorgeous for this sweater, you're crazy, Bernard, gold, and what next? with what money.

Then The Owl straightened up, turned to Woodsmoke and shot him a murderous look,

It's gorgeous all right, oh yeah, it sure is gorgeous.

And then Evelyne sobbing almost, her voice trembling and begging,

We helped you as much as we could, we did, and you, how, how could you,

And Woodsmoke no longer smiling, straightening up:

It's for Solange, for her. That's nobody's business but hers.

And it was much later, at the end of the afternoon, with the gendarmes and the mayor, that Patou, sitting down at one of the tables in the back room of her bar smoking cigarette after cigarette, would tell how Woodsmoke had arrived at her bar after the incident of the brooch. She had no idea that one day she would be sitting there for him.

What she said: he just didn't have a clue. He really wanted to do the best he could, for weeks he'd been thinking about his present. In fact he'd already talked about it, she said. But like always we must have let him talk, and to go along with him slipped a little *yes* into his speech here and there that we didn't even hear ourselves say.

Yes, Woodsmoke. A brooch, yes, Woodsmoke. Your sister will be happy, yes, it's great, yes, a brooch, great.

While she rinsed the glasses and served this one and that one, workers for lunch or youngsters at the pool table, just to go along with his monologue,

Yes, Woodsmoke,

But not really listening when he said he went to the jeweler's, to Buchet's.

Whereas it was Monsieur Buchet himself who had come out of the back room where he was working, because his wife had called him right away, even before Woodsmoke had walked through the door, much less spoken, as he was waiting for a customer to pay up and then leave.

He stood there smiling for a rather long moment, his hands fiddling with his cap, probably looking rather dumb or childish, with the face and eyes he had, even if his build was too thick, his body too coarse to make you think of childhood when you saw him in his orange sweater with big holes in it—or even of

the image one has of childhood, shyness and childish awkward-
ness. And if he was puerile, it was more in the way he took the
fat yellow envelope out of the pocket of his parka and pulled off
the red rubber band to lay out a thick wad of two hundred franc
bills on the counter.

The jeweler and his wife will talk about that to the gendarmes:
the bills on the counter, and Woodsmoke's voice,

Here, it's for a brooch.

The couple must have looked at each other and divided the
tasks without saying anything, taking the treasures out of their
boxes for him, presenting a few trays lined with black or blue
velvet with the finest jewelry shining on them, see, we have all
kinds, and his wife running off quickly to slip a bill into one
of those machines to check if they had fakes in front of them
or real money (all that money he'd left on the counter disdain-
fully, without paying any attention to it, him, a poor slob, a
bum), and even, perhaps, incredulously rubbing them, feeling them, checking them one last time under the gleam of an
electric light before glancing at her husband, no problem, it's
real. Monsieur Buchet may also have reported Woodsmoke's
doubts when he'd hesitated a long time between two brooches,
finally giving up on the gold beetle, to the despair of Madame
Buchet, because she knew that the stench of men like him
becomes embedded in things like the smell of dog-hair wet
from the rain; she must have cursed that golden beetle as well
as her husband who made his hesitation last instead of inciting
him to get it over with, yes, let's get it over with, let him pay
and clear off, him and his brooch and whatever remains of his
huge roll of bills, but especially his filth and stink, that stench
it would take weeks, for sure, no doubt about it, weeks to get
rid of completely.

It was nighttime now, since night takes over in December as soon as afternoon ends, sometimes a little before the end of the afternoon in fact, very early, very dark. Outside, I could see the snow dancing in big flakes alternately blue and orange, because the Christmas decorations lit up the whole length of the avenue.

What Patou told the gendarmes, the mayor, and me too, was yes of course she knew about the money.

Nobody was in the café. Jean-Marc was behind the bar. Sometimes a car would stop in front of the entrance, someone would pop out of the passenger door and bolt in, saying hello and complaining about the weather. Jean-Marc would sell them cigarettes and the car would leave again immediately. Then he'd walk back toward us with the packet of cold air the customer had let in on his way out the door. Jean-Marc wasn't the talkative type. Sometimes he would nod when Patou raised her eyes to him for support, and we heard him repeat yes he knew and Patou knew, too, because Woodsmoke had told them, didn't hide it, as he was paying his slate cash on the nail with one hundred and two hundred franc bills, crumpled and kind of stale, she'd added (yes, she insisted, the bills were old). He told them a whole lot of money had just come in. As much money as his coffin could hold. No, not his, of course. Not his own coffin. She'd corrected herself, when suddenly I cut in,

His mother, it's his mother's money.

That's what went through my mind. His mother. Not only didn't that money drop from heaven but he'd gone to get it, he helped himself, yes, that's it, at his mother's, when three months earlier Solange and Evelyne came to pick up the Old Lady at her house to take her to the rest home. Before they took the few things she wanted to bring with her, and above all before they locked up the house. That's probably when he came, as he was the only one still living near La Migne, or what remained of it, it was easy to go in, comb through the place, empty the closets and look for the money she must have stashed away somewhere, in a shoebox, or out back, in the barn, inside the cement stalls, where they used to kill the pig.

Because there are good hiding places there. Unless it was simply under her bed, or between the boards of her wardrobe.

He'd found it.

And that was exactly like him, so much like him, robbing his own mother as if to get back what he felt was owed him, whereas the day she left he had showed up and just stood there a few meters up the hill without saying anything, watching her go off to the old people's home with no possibility of ever returning to the place she'd always lived, as if now he was the sole owner of the place, the last heir of a long line—end of the century, end of the race, end of the end—but with his eyes sharp and his determination clear and set, all the more fixed and wicked as it was the culmination of several centuries of mud and field work and for him, surely, of the humiliation and exploitation of all of them by one woman, all bent over, dressed in black, with her light blue eyes like teeth biting her territory, her old sick house and the shed across from it, on the other side of the street.

Rabut?

Yes, sorry. I was thinking about his mother.

He doesn't like you very much.

No, I don't think so.

And then she told how he'd come in a little while ago, right after the thing with the brooch.

They'd seen him cross the street without watching for cars, at the beginning of the afternoon then, maybe around one thirty or a little later. He didn't say anything when he walked into the café, didn't stop at the bar or even look in that direction, unlike what he usually did. He had crossed the first room and then chose to sit at the back, at a table near the wall and the juke box. Patou had come up to him, surprised to see him there already. He said he was hungry and didn't answer when she asked him why he didn't stay to have lunch with the others.

She suspected he'd have to eat and drink for his tongue to loosen up and his eyes to open so they could finally look in front of them for somebody to talk to, if only to pour out the words that must have been knocking around in his head, and she had seen, guessed, imagined those words clashing and attacking as she watched him chewing on the potatoes as if they were over-cooked meat.

Because he'd eaten and drunk very quickly.

All of a sudden he had wanted to say what rankled him, what was weighing on his heart, a heart so heavy it was close to exploding in his throat, as he said when he began to speak; you see, he said, explode in my throat from, pouring himself more wine and gulping down throatfuls big enough to drown two or three litters of kittens. Still chewing while he spoke, biting into the bread, the potatoes and the herring, indifferent to the spectacle he was making of himself, as if he himself didn't see it, as if he had no part in it and didn't know he was obscene, dirty, repulsive too, swallowing the way he did and letting the oil line his mouth and chin with its thick, sticky, shining matter. But he wasn't an ogre either, not a monster, just a guy with anger rising in him to replace the incomprehension and feeling of injustice, scorn and hatred he felt had victimized him.

Because really, they'd known him such a loudmouth, so haughty, and now it was as if a spring in him had broken from being stretched too much, wound up too much, and had given way to something wavering, dancing in the blue of his eyes, when he looked at you or you thought he was looking at you but you weren't sure, you just imagined it was a look because of a slight insistence, a murky stare despite the blinking of his eyelids.

And that's how he must have spoken to Patou and told how upset he'd been seeing Solange take off the brooch, and the others, the brothers and sisters, seeing them converge on her like the birds of prey they all were, scenting money, all that money, as if they owned it and what's more, as if they owned him, too, a bunch of dumb hicks who never saw Paris except in pictures or on their TV screen, who never saw anything but the water of the river and the ponds slimy as fuel oil where the cows used to drink when they were kids.

Yes. His scorn. His scorn for them. His anger.

And Patou told how at times she had to get up to serve someone at the bar or in the front room, and he'd keep quiet, she said, and drink, coffee, brandy, wine, then some more brandy, then wine again, then he'd mumble and look through the glass door to catch sight of the people coming out of the community hall, because now the aperitif was over; the tables must have been set up for lunch and they probably had started serving.

Then he stood up. He had walked to the bar, not looking straight in front of him but with his head bent toward the outside, to the other side of the sidewalk across the street, seeing only the door and over it the big façade painted yellow. That's what he was looking at. When he took out a cigarette,

Hey, give me another. Glass of red.

And then the time to say,

    They've always been so fucking jealous.

And the worst of it, she said when the mayor suggested that he must have premeditated the whole thing—the provocation, staging the scene—is that no, I swear to God, no, I'm sure of it, he was convinced nobody would have a problem with it.

    She even went on by telling how, if she had a doubt now, it was because of her that he had fallen so easily into a rage. True, he was already very close to falling into a rage because of all the alcohol he'd drunk, and he was drinking all the more easily because he was getting dizzy hearing himself tell her—her, Patou—everything that rankled him: for example, eliminating through words the humiliation she hadn't witnessed, the humiliation he felt when Solange had taken off the brooch and her sisters and brothers—not all of them, it's true OK, but still they formed the first circle and the others came over and stood around them, the others were there too, against him, to see and hear how they were going to blame him, like the youngest one, Evelyne, whining, sobbing, After all we did for you.

And she'd been the first to talk about the Old Lady. She'd said: mother.

    You came to rob the Old Lady.

    And Solange in one breath,

    That's enough now,

    And again,

    Be quiet.

As for him, he'd retreated without saying a thing. He let them talk. He let them go on, like he always did. Like every time the wind rises. A squall, there's a squall. That's what he'd thought and didn't say, not yet, just retreating with his hands in his pockets, boring his way through all the hostile looks and bodies around him, hostile or just dumb, stupid bodies who came to have a look, he'd walked out, and outside, quickly crossed the street and dove into Patou's, on this side of the street.

And she looked at Jean-Marc when the gendarmes said it was serious. Afterwards, she wanted to smile and pour another glass of wine. And as if to change the subject, she asked me,

Tell me, Rabut, I wanted to ask you this for years, how come he calls you the graduate? What's the story with that?

I saw her hand shake as she filled the glasses to the brim. All I did was smile, yes, there is a story.

Nothing at all, just something between him and me. I would have liked to go on with school and he thought the idea of going to high school was pretentious. You have to realize that at the time, going to high school . . . And then, here, in this place, me, one of his cousins. You have no idea. Of course I never graduated high school. I never had the chance. But he always thought it was funny that I could even think of it.

What I said to Patou: It's kind of a joke between the two of us.

She didn't pick up on it, she had asked just to say something. Because the same idea must still have been bothering her, an idea she would always have when she went over that day in her memory: she had stirred up his hatred when she wanted to make him understand how provocative it was, what he had done, in a situation where his naiveté couldn't be understood, not by anybody, and certainly not by them, his brothers and sisters.

She wanted to make him understand, that's all. Understand first their astonishment, and then the idea that he'd stolen money from their mother when the question of paying for the rest home had come up and they were discussing it, each of them agreeing to pay more so he would have nothing to lay out. And three months later they saw him throw money out the window—their windows—their money right under their eyes.

That's what he'd done.

Woodsmoke, you got to understand them. Except for one or two, they don't have much money.

And he hadn't replied, and he'd left. Patou's voice had remained hanging in the air, the way chemical particles you can't see dissolve and become nothing in the open air and the blue of the sky. They had looked at him through the glass door. As usual, he spat on the sidewalk as he crossed over, staggering, more drunk than they thought. And more frightening, too. Because they must have been slightly scared then. Certainly more than they told us, the gendarmes, the mayor and me, only three hours later.

But they must have said to themselves: Woodsmoke is Woodsmoke and he's drunk, you're not going to change him, it's the way he usually is, that's all.

So, when he walked in, that is, not exactly at the moment he crossed the threshold, but when everyone realized, saw, began to see, a certain silence set in, a tremor in the silence and laughs, too, a few laughs; and then the people who still hadn't seen anything and kept on doing whatever they'd been doing.

Solange wasn't there, she was in the kitchen. Woodsmoke walked toward us with a decided but unsteady step. He must have gotten completely drunk and was coming back like an alcoholic who thinks he has to explain himself when in fact all he's doing is muddling his own ideas as well as other people's. I saw The Owl nudge Jean-Jacques with her elbow, probably scandalized that her brother-in-law would dare to return, and Jean-Jacques hesitantly murmuring,

So . . . what do you want me to do about it?

And then Evelyne got up. She walked very fast with her head down, not looking at anybody, letting her high heels clack on the floor, pulling on her funny-colored sweater—melon juice or salmon pink—to occupy her hands and compose herself, the time to walk by the stage and go into the kitchen to warn Solange.

But already he had come over to us.

He planted himself in the middle of the hall—no, not in the middle of the hall but near the stage, at the center of the three huge tables they'd put together in the shape of a U—and he stayed like that for a few minutes, struggling to remain upright, standing bow-legged, or rather with his legs spread apart and a fixed, transparent stare, distant, scornful, and already looking like he was provoking us, expecting from us answers to questions that may have been hanging in the air for centuries.

And of course all eyes were on him. Of course you could begin to hear murmuring. Everybody sat there looking at him, drinking their glass of wine, pouring themselves another or on the contrary emptying it in one gulp. You could hear some laughs.

Low voices, whispers.

Wants to be the center of attention.

Won't fall down.

Don't pay attention to him. Don't pay any attention.

And they passed the salt or pepper or water or wine. They wiped their hands with paper napkins. Others were chewing pieces of bread, then glancing at him. Don't pay any attention to him. That's what he wants, attention. Don't look at him. Nicole asked me,

But what's Solange doing?

And The Owl's feet fidgeting under her chair. And the voices of the old ladies, at the end of the table. Or the voice of a brother who never spoke, hardly ever, in from his fields where he spent his time growing beets and corn and who suddenly yelled,

Woodsmoke, that's enough, come and sit down!

And there he was, rocking slightly from side to side, just quivering, reeling a little, with the tips of his feet moving like in a dance, a tiny little movement of the soles forward and back, and always, that scorn in his eyes. He looked at his brother, the one who'd spoken, and didn't answer. As if the voice had only reached him filtered through something other than hearing or intelligence; and then a doubt, his chest, his neck, his head raised, yes, he said, at first so weakly that it would have been impossible to understand the stammered, hardly pronounced words if we hadn't heard them already, mumbled, repeated the way drunks repeat the same words, the same obsessions over and over.

It started with mangled words, or rather words planed down and skipped over, a smooth, continuous wave, without consonants or vowels to form identifiable sounds, but we knew them, I knew them, since we'd heard them in the past, forever—no, not really forever—we knew the litany stammered through his lips,

Oh, they're talking to me, hey, they're talking to me, yeah, I bet there's a crowd here, hey, they're all here, oh no, not the dead ones, the dead didn't come, they didn't come, great, that many less here, it makes for that many less, good, that many less, Reine and the dead kids didn't come, too bad, the dead kids were the only ones worth a damn, right, and my sister, where's Solange, my sister, where'd she go.

His voice suddenly stopping, ending in a crash, turning into a look of scorn for me.

Hey, the graduate. With his lady graduate.

A laugh. Or rather a kind of laugh, a splutter, a little giggle quickly smothered.

Then silence.

Then his voice, very loud, that came from deep inside himself to scare us perhaps, but mostly directed at Solange, who was taking a long time to return, what could Solange be doing in that kitchen.

It's her party and she's the one in the kitchen, you're not ashamed of yourselves letting her do everything in her kitchen, you bunch of loafers, hey, the graduate over there, what do you think?

Then he spoke louder and louder, his voice shaking but not halting, not at all, not hesitating even for a second when he latched on to the syllables of his sister's name, drawing on it, finding in it the strength to hold on and climb back up as if with his hands, with both hands, with his voice breaking yet loud,

Solange, where the hell is Solange?

It's true, she wasn't coming, taking a long time to return, and when she finally came, when she came back towards us, along with Pingeot and Chefraoui, one with wine, the other with a stainless steel platter of roasted meats, Bernard walked toward the entrance to the kitchen. Slowly, with determination. Chefraoui with his metal platter. The platters they had borrowed, Solange and him, from the school cafeteria where they'd been co-workers for years, serving meals to the children.

And then.

Because Chefraoui was there all of sudden, in front of him, in his field of vision. Like an impossible image that had surged up to blur reality. Chefraoui was smiling or wasn't smiling, it doesn't matter. It's impossible to know. But we already know. We've known all along. Since, I mean—ever since—but that's something else, that time back there. Just something, something I'm thinking, which slips in and blurs this moment of our personal history when all of a sudden it's there, like a forty-year-old score to settle, forty years, the age of a mature man, when we look at ourselves and tell ourselves no, it's not over, we thought it was over but it wasn't.

Then Woodsmoke's voice said very loudly, calling to Solange,

What about him. *He* can be here. He has the right to be here, the. He's got the right but me, me . . .

Solange dropped the things she was holding on the table, we heard the crash of metal on the thick board that vibrated on the trestles.

Bernard, stop it.

But *he's* got the right to be here. Him, the.

Stop.

That dirty sonofabitch, the fuckin' Arab–

Solange wouldn't let him finish. She jumped toward him and yelled his name, Bernard, Bernard you're not gonna go on like that get out of here right now get out and she had tears in her eyes and a broken voice, with Chefraoui standing there without saying anything, dumfounded, and she turned to him, distraught and ashamed,

Saïd, don't pay attention to him, it's nothing.

Chefraoui didn't answer. He just put the platter down in the middle of the table and held out the silverware to the nearest guest so he could help himself, and that was about it.

He didn't bat an eyelid, his face didn't move. You couldn't see any expression on it.

And for a second, barely, it looked like nothing more would happen and Woodsmoke would retreat.

But his body swung forward and his arms, which had been spread wide, moved all the way in front of him, his hands not closed into fists yet but on the contrary open like hungry animals he had no way of controlling, scared himself to see them free, powerful, acting that way, stretching out until they were close to Chefraoui who backed up, surprised, you could see his irritation, his anger, he backed up some more, not slightly but resolutely this time, a few steps away, almost in disgust, not be touched by Bernard's hands, repulsive, the smell of ash even under his black fingernails—how can you stink of wood smoke like that—and that filth, those fingernails, those patches of bright pink, raw skin, and that stench almost more appalling now than the gesture of those hands thrusting forward. But also his stare. But also the body swinging forward.

But also the words.

You fuckin' Arab sonofabitch. For years I wanted to say that to you. I'm gonna tell you. And I felt like knocking your block off. Fuckin' Arab.

Stop it.

Stop.

He wasn't listening to anything anymore now. Solange suddenly putting herself between the two men and pushing Woodsmoke away without even thinking,

Come on, that's enough, and now get out of here, Bernard, just get out, Rabut, help me.

And behind us voices, other voices, voices of women, men, the brothers and the cousins, voices whose timbre, intonation and accents we knew by heart, voices that came flying over the tables to put a stop to the scene, defuse the tension, calm things down,

Hey Woodsmoke, cut the crap, we don't talk about Arabs like that here,

Get it Woodsmoke,
Woodsmoke,
You weren't always that fussy about Arabs, were you.

And apparently waking up suddenly and turning away from his target, the time to spot who'd spoken.
Who said that?
Turning his head,
Who said that?
The French, the French back there, they weren't Arabs.

That lasted a second. And for a second there was this funny silence, something like that feeling of embarrassment when you come upon someone who's naked: the trembling in Woodsmoke's voice and the image of the woman he had loved in the far-off time when Woodsmoke had not yet erased Bernard.

It lasted a second, hardly a second.

He hesitated another second then he regained his breath, glanced around, looking for something to lean on, unsteady like an alcoholic when he's thinking, and staggers more in his head than in his body, when he has a moment of wavering, of going back over himself, perhaps. And then suddenly in front of him Solange, who was there with the little deep blue box in her hand.
Take this and get the hell out.
No.
Take it, take it, Bernard, I don't want to see your face anymore.
And for a brief moment, he thought she was joking. For a moment he actually thought they wouldn't really order him to leave. And yet she demanded that he leave. Chefraoui didn't

budge. He stayed slightly in the background. And I walked toward them, a few steps. Nicole too. And others too. Jean-Jacques and The Owl. Evelyne already crying.

Then Woodsmoke looked at the blue box Solange had shaken in her hand in front of him, for him to take it, take it back, take it once and for all and make it disappear and let's forget about it, let's not talk about it anymore, never again.

And the money. You gonna tell us where the money comes from?

The Owl had almost shouted yes, exactly at that moment, when all we were waiting for now was for Woodsmoke to leave. Because we could feel he'd lost his grip, he was losing his footing, finally the dikes were going to give way inside him and leave him emptied of his aggressiveness and his need to lash out. But there was The Owl's voice. And the ones that hadn't said anything yet—outraged more by the business with the money, with the brooch, than by the scandal of the insults—joined in, raising their voices, demanding answers,

Woodsmoke, who did you steal that from? who? where does it come from? answer, you got to tell us, you got to,

And he didn't answer.

Whose money is it?

He was looking at his sister,

Answer me.

He looked at the deep blue box,

Just tell us.

His eyes, through which he had never seen anything but the desert of his solitude, were empty and transparent. He remained quiet for a moment, frozen, then suddenly he raised his head and looked at them all, acting as if he were answering each of them with a nod, holding his chin high, with nothing but scorn for an answer; and then his precipitation when he stretched out his arm to grab whatever fell beneath his hand, a glass of wine, a glass almost full that he grabbed and threw in front of him, just the contents because at first he kept the glass in his hand before throwing it far enough to reach the other end, and the glass broke, of course—but more than shattering glass there was the shattering of voices, how they all stood up and how we saw the wine and the stains spattered on Chefraoui but also on Solange, on her white and yellow chiné sweater.

Then it all went very fast. The men rushed him.

And Solange, paralyzed for a moment, alone in the midst of all her guests, drowned among them and tossed about for a few more minutes, the time to see us (I was standing back a little, my body refusing to move forward, impossible to lay a hand on Woodsmoke, impossible for me), and the others, a few others, cousins, friends, the deathly pale face and tearful eyes of Solange, pathetic with her miserable expression, her distraught face and her stained sweater that she'll have to go change, as much to be alone and maybe cry as to react, put up a good show, come back and start going again despite everything, despite that bad moment of seeing them all crowding around Woodsmoke and forcing him to leave, while he resists—but without shouting, without a word, trying to hit, collapsing while they pull him by the arms, by his jacket, and Woodsmoke, with the strength of inertia and his punches too, he lands a few punches but no one dares hit him, he's too strong, too stubborn, they know he'd remember, he'd be able to recognize the author of each blow and they're afraid of him when they drag him out, throw him out, closing the door behind him and leaving him on the landing, alone, with that mean face and thick mass, that bull's neck, retreating, but with his scorn still, up to the end, up to the moment when on the landing he stood up and looked at us, without moving, without a word.

Then he left.

And after that there was a time of uncertainty, with Solange absent for a good half hour. And then that part of the meal without her. Finally, her return and the departure of Chefraoui and Pingeot.

And then, at the end of the afternoon, or rather at the beginning of the evening, they arrived.

Night had fallen and the snow had started to fall again, even harder than over the last twenty-four hours. The mayor and the gendarmes. I'm the one they came to see.

Because first of all, I'm on the city council, but also because I'm a member of the North Africa Veterans Association and I know everybody around here, Chefraoui and his wife, but mostly because I'm Woodsmoke's cousin.

But really. With their uneasiness at interrupting a family meal. How could they imagine I could listen to them without flinching as they asked me to do, and that I could believe things had gone so far, so —

Well, no, that's not the way I should tell it.

Not the way things landed on me or the way I had to face them, when the mayor suggested we sit down in the kitchen and talk.

But to say what.

To say, yes, I can see Woodsmoke very well, furious and drunk on his moped, and maybe more awake too, stung by the cold and the snow slapping his face, going back to his place and slowing down when in the distance, on the other side of the fields going up the slope of La Migne, he saw the three or four new houses and Chefraoui's house among them.

To say, yes, Mayor, that must be it.

I can see the landscape clearly, completely white, or actually a faded grayish white like stale bread, shapeless, with little houses drowning in the thick, soft sky, and underneath, the fields, the woods hard as marble and brittle, a long triangle of bare earth covered with white going up towards La Migne, and down below, the Old Lady's house, smoke from chimneys stirring an oily gray into the dust-gray of the clouds, and him out there in the cold, all red, purplish almost, with his shoulders whitened, and the moped, the helmet, everything, and his eyes fixed for a moment on the other side. That's what you have to see. What they were asking me to see. Woodsmoke hesitating. And what I had to tell myself: he stopped on his moped, and probably, for a fraction of a second, a handful of seconds thrown into the air, he felt a vague desire for vengeance. That's the idea the mayor and the gendarmes had wanted me to hear.

I said: wait, wait a minute. I want to understand. Tell me from the start. That's what you think? You think he came back and went to Chefraoui's house?

An idea like that, from him? No.

That's what happened.

No.

I'm telling you.

He's crazy but he wouldn't.

And they told me how he'd made a U-turn on his moped and rode back down towards the fork in the road, they saw him from Rondot's place, you know how Rondot spends his whole life at the window, he saw him in the middle of the road up there, going back up to his place with the snow falling hard, and stopping in the middle of the road, all alone, like that, for no reason, then making a U-turn and going back down past Rondot's house actually, not to go back towards the town but to take another road, toward the new houses. Rondot saw him go by, hesitate again just before he turned, and look to see if anyone was coming. It all fits. And what about that business this afternoon, Rabut,

What business?

Something about jewels or whatever.

Who told you that?

Chefraoui. Come on Rabut, you're not going to.

No, not a chance, but still wait a minute.

Wait for what?

What happened, said Ménard, the head of the gendarmes, is how Chefraoui went to the station at the end of the afternoon.

He told me that he, Ménard, when he got to the police station, he'd found Chefraoui with his hands on his knees sitting on one of the chairs in front of the reception desk. Jamain was typing some report or other, as if, in a town of four thousand people, he was used to seeing a man barge into the police station, so upset, and stunned too, seemingly numb from not really believing what he'd seen, what he'd come to report.

And so, seeing him sitting there so calm—or rather so docile—with a kind of fatalism which made him repeat over and over that if he hadn't promised his daughter to come back home early to share the birthday cake, God knows what would have happened, he'd repeated, and with that other guy typing some useless report that could have, should have, waited—that moment had been unbearable for Ménard; and that's all it took to make him angry with Jamain, but maybe a little with Chefraoui, too. And Ménard hardly had the time to ask Jamain if he'd taken down Chefraoui's contact info, if he'd maybe offered him a glass of water, a cup of coffee, something, if he'd notified whoever and done what needed to be done, what one is supposed to do (and incidentally, Ménard was annoyed because of the time his subordinate had probably taken before daring to "bother" him, as he put it: "I'm sorry to bother you during your break, sir, but there's this . . . ," etc.) when Chefraoui was already up from his chair and walking over to Ménard, apologizing for bothering him on a Saturday. Yes, *he* was apologizing, at a time like that.

Chefraoui's calm.

Chefraoui's voice telling me to come. To come right away. I should come, Ménard said, because I had to arrest the madman.

And it was hard to understand words pronounced only to ward off fear and certainly not so that Ménard—with his little mustache and his slightly hollow cheeks, his crew cut, no matter how important he was, with his rank, his mottoes, his Republic and his jail cells that were only used for sobering up a few morons too drunk to drive home, or teenagers caught breaking into summer homes—certainly not so that he, Ménard, could give him an answer and do something about that fear Chefraoui knew was on him like a face that had replaced his own.

Wait a minute, I don't get it.

What, Rabut, what is it you don't get?

You're telling me that Woodsmoke.

Chefraoui told us what happened that afternoon. How your cousin drank too much and the scene he made. We want to know if you can confirm.

Wait a minute, if I can confirm. If I. That. You want me to. Me to tell you. And for me to confirm yes, here, what happened here. We're not going to talk about that, not here, it's impossible, we're not going to.

No.

I suggested we continue the conversation at Patou's. There, we sat down and started talking again. We ordered coffee, Patou and Jean-Marc didn't dare ask us why we were there, two gendarmes and the mayor and me at this time of day, with a worried look, probably so worried it was scary.

It was only afterwards, when we had agreed among us as to what we should do, that we asked Patou to join us. But for the moment, we were talking softly, whispering almost. We were talking, I was listening to Ménard telling how they'd taken the police car to go to the premises. And you could feel the irritation still lingering in his voice, his restrained anger at Chefraoui because strangely, he hadn't been so cooperative, no, because he was so damn discreet, so silent, like a dead weight, just rehashing that bit about how lucky it was, that piece of luck, his daughter's birthday or else he'd never have come back home so early.

And, Ménard said, I lost my temper at him in the car, to make him talk, tell us, and it came out as a whisper, as if he was scared of what he was saying.

I ran, I tried to hold him back.

There was blood, I saw blood.

And Ménard had to tell how Woodsmoke's smell had hit him as soon as he reached the door. You could still smell it. That stench there, so strong that since he couldn't find anything to say to Chefraoui when he got out, he had to ask how he heated the house. And it took some time before he could answer and let out, for all reply,

It's *his* smell.

And Ménard talked. Ménard's voice telling not what he'd seen, but what Chefraoui had found when he got back from the party.

He told how Chefraoui had entered his yard, cautiously, because the entrance through the gate isn't that wide, especially in snowy weather. And then behind the rows of thujas, behind the white gate diluted in the whiteness of the snow, he'd seen the yard, that yard all white, too, and at the back, lying almost under the stairs, Woodsmoke's moped.

Chefraoui had hesitated a moment, not to get out of his car—on the contrary, he probably did that fast because he had no reason to find the moped there. He hesitated because he wasn't sure what to do, what he should do, run up into his house, rush in and beat Woodsmoke to it, get him unawares, jump on him like that, by force, throw all his strength into it, his arms and back tensed, lean over the drunk and grab him by the collar and without talking, drag him to the door then throw him out, with the risk of his falling down the stairs, smashing up, breaking his head and bones, crashing all the way down to the yard where the snow would finally wake him and sober him up or kill him completely and not tell himself he might resist, Woodsmoke is strong, even drunk he could put up resistance, but if you take him by surprise maybe, or maybe not, or on the contrary be prudent, on your guard.

But not imagine anything worse, that's what Chefraoui must have thought to reassure himself, to tell himself it's something unpleasant and nothing more; it couldn't be, it can't be anything more.

And the moped Bernard hadn't bothered to keep upright on its kickstand and had fallen down, he'd just found it lying on one of its saddlebags, the wheels not turning in the air but motionless, stopped, and the snow had already covered them with a thin lumpy film of shapeless confetti, all too white—that was only a sign of haste and clumsiness due to liquor, nothing more, no more than that, and not the blindness, the determination, the relentlessness of a man who knows what he wants to do and is going to do it, quickly, with no restraint.

So Chefraoui went up to the house, not the way he usually did by going through the basement, but through the front entrance, taking the stairs like the other one must have done, probably, he did the same thing and then at the moment of going up the steps Woodsmoke had climbed before him, Chefraoui felt fear coming over him, more and more with each step, the blood in his head and even the strange heat of fear clashing with the outside cold, up to the moment he put his hand on the doorknob.

His heart beating, knocking, hammering, then silence. That's what he said. That silence. The moment he opened. His stupefaction at finding the door locked. Having to grope for the key in his pocket and open up. The time to tremble and watch himself go through the motion of putting the key in the lock and turning it, then putting it back in his pocket (he, who almost never used it). He could have called his wife, the kids, or even just the dog. He looked at the key and was surprised not to be able to call out. He walked into his house, slowly, very slowly, despite the smell, so aggressive, so sour, of charred wood, soon of charcoal, reeking, mixed with the lingering odor of liquor.

He remained frozen in his tracks for a moment, without moving. Very intent, very erect. He held his breath for a second, then he walked.

First, the hallway. And the silence. The ticking of the clock in the kitchen, and the kitchen, there, just to the right, he didn't go in but looked just enough to notice it was tidy, the dishes dried and put away, the sideboard empty and wiped clean, the oilcloth on the table and the saucers and that box for the birthday candles, and the mail on the fridge, the rainbow reflection of the liquor bottles and the round traces of the dishrag on the kitchen furniture.

And the silence, still.

Still the silence as he passed the door to the cellar stairs. He kept going. He turned left, without accelerating, without listening to the voice inside him that told him to run and shout the names of his wife and kids, that voice, more timid, not giving in to panic, but also perhaps more surprised that the dog hadn't come up to him and hadn't barked. He was walking slowly and his steps sounded inside him like the ideas passing before his eyes, as unstable as the snow outside.

The doors to the toilet and the bathroom, on the left, closed. The door to his bedroom across the hall, too, like his daughter's door.

Only the boys' bedroom was open.

And that's where he found the three of them. The girl sitting on the edge of the bed with the youngest boy huddled in her arms; the oldest was standing with his back turned to him, looking out the window. He ran up to them and they threw themselves into his arms, all three of them—no, not all three, not the oldest, who just made a motion to turn around and then immediately went back to stare far into the garden, at a precise spot his eyes couldn't move away from, were not able to leave, while the two others were running up to their father.

The girl—she turned thirteen yesterday—stubborn, obstinate, unable to let go of her little brother, to stop stroking his hair and as if to reassure herself whisper to him that everything's ok, everything's ok he's going to leave, he's going to get out of the house and mommy,

Mommy,

Chefraoui letting go of his hug and not listening to the voice of the little one when he whispered that he was afraid, and the heavy, insistent caresses of his sister, her body rocking as if in prayer,

It's ok, it's going to be ok, everything's ok, he's going to leave, he's going to get out of the house and mommy,

Mommy,

Chefraoui going over to the window and suddenly, at the moment he was close and just before he could see, or even make out what his son was looking at with such intensity, he heard the moped in the yard—you could hear the effort, the pedals chugging to start it up, but with this cold it wasn't starting.

And Chefraoui didn't think, didn't hesitate either, he ran to the door and without hesitation threw himself outside without even thinking about the cold, the whiteness of the snow and its reverberation blinding for a moment, a very brief instant, when just under the stairs, leaning over the moped that he'd picked up and set on the stand where it was balanced, the back wheel raised, turning in the air—Woodsmoke, leaning forward and pedaling standing up almost so the gas and the engine, so you could hear the engine, the few little explosions and the smoke behind the muffler, and then Woodsmoke raised his head and saw Chefraoui above him on the stoop of the house, Chefraoui furious this time, looking at him. The moped started up, it leaves its stand and skids on the snow, the brake Woodsmoke hadn't tightened, the wheel turning too fast, too hard, the moped touching the ground while the wheel is free, it sends the moped flying too fast, zigzagging, Woodsmoke trying to take control again with his arms tensed and his torso leaning back, but Chefraoui is almost upon him, he touches his arm, the thick blood sticks to his hand and Woodsmoke quickly puts his foot on the ground and pushes with his heel to pull the engine that misfires, slows down, hesitates, bogged down in the snow, the holes, pebbles flying, some clacking like lead on the metal of the car, white smoke behind the muffler and Chefraoui's hand closed on Woodsmoke's arm and the shouts, a few shouts drowned under the shouting of the engine, but the momentum is stronger now, Woodsmoke is stronger now, he's almost leaning at a right angle to pick up speed, Chefraoui has to run, stretch out his arms and try to kick at the saddlebags to destabilize the moped, make it waver and shake, leave its trajectory, in vain.

And it's only afterwards that he'll understand how Woodsmoke had first walked into the house through the stairs without knocking, finding himself alone for a moment, with his revolting smell invading the whole space around him. As if he had touched the whole space and taken it over.

Chefraoui's wife had appeared suddenly. Or, no. Not even that. She had only realized that someone had just come into her house without warning, without knocking, someone whose moped and footsteps on the stairs she had heard, and the cold and the wind had come with him, well before the stench. She thought right away of her husband, then she told herself no, it wasn't her husband.

These are things you know instinctively, you guess them, the presence of a stranger.

She'd told the children to stay in the bedroom, not to budge. And they hadn't budged. Even when they heard their mother's voice asking the stranger what he was doing there and heard him answer, but not right away, he hadn't answered right away, he had stayed there without saying anything, silent, leaving her still more surprised.

And from the bedroom, what the children must have thought is that the man hadn't come to talk, he'd come for something they knew nothing about but were afraid of right away, especially the little one, because his sister and brother held him back when he wanted to go to his mother, saying,

No, don't move,

the sister thinking it wise to stick her hand tight over his lips. The man spoke and at first they didn't understand what the voice was saying. A voice without pronunciation, without syllables; a voice talking in a choppy language that sometimes rose, got carried away, shouted then suddenly collapsed and seemed to go out or slump into an interminable, creepy, crawling sneer.

And that lasted a very long time. They thought it was lasting an infinitely long time, because sometimes there were those silences, like a lull in time, dead angles, only silence—that is, nothing, a hole, as if it were over and had never begun.

Then the voice would start up again. Or their mother's voice. Or neither of their voices, but a breath or a shifting, a movement they recognized right away as not being their mother's but something thick, violent. Such an infinitely long time. They didn't say anything and the sister and the older brother hardly looked at each other or tried to find in the other one the answers and confirmations of their ideas whose trace was immediately erased by a shout; they were straining their ears and wondering who was behind the voice, who the stranger was, what did the stranger want, when the mother's voice suddenly seemed amplified; it reached them in their room to warm them up a little and reassure them. Because they heard the door open.

OK, get out now.

Then they imagined their mother leaning over the stranger and even grabbing him to push him out, since the door was open, they'd heard it, the door had been opened and the cold had even swept into the bedroom, nipping at their feet in slippers and their faces, at the hand over the little brother's mouth. And finally the door closing. A turn of the key. And the hand relaxing its grip. The fingers loosening; the imprint of the fingers on the reddened skin of the little brother. And then suddenly their mother in front of them, furious and haggard at the same time, satisfied to have made the intruder leave and still surprised, not frightened but angry.

Who was that?

There was no response from her. Her eyes, distraught, on her children. On the head of the little one, who had come over to snuggle up to her for comfort. And her daughter's voice,

Who was that?

The voice of her oldest son.

Who was that?

She didn't answer right away and opened her eyes very wide, her face suddenly on the alert and anxious, like them.

Be quiet.

And the little one on the contrary holding out his arms, pressing against her, mumbling, whining, his sister saying be quiet it's over it's ok and then her,

Shhh, be quiet.

The older brother looking at his mother, then turning around and glancing out the window and seeing the dog, the dog rushing toward the cellar.

Be quiet, he's here.

He's not gone.

And then the dog barked.

Relentlessly, without stopping. And Chefraoui's wife ordered her children to stay there, all three of them, and not to move.

He's not gone.

She went to the kitchen and there, from her window, she saw the moped on the ground, and the snow dancing on the gray of the sky. The silence of the snow and that slowness when on the contrary the dog was barking, bellowing louder and louder, becoming almost threatening.

The noises, the door opening.

And suddenly sounds of metal, of wood, of objects banging against each other and falling. Metal and wood against the cement. And the dog keeping it up, jumping, the dog suddenly furious. That's what she thought: the dog was furious and maybe he was going to bite. She could not think of what to do. She pictured the man down there. And it was as if his stench had annihilated any possibility of thinking, reasoning, or acting. That must have lasted for quite a while. How much time in the kitchen, without moving. Looking at the snow covering the moped. Hearing the dog's barking. The things falling, being shoved around.

All of a sudden the dog didn't bark anymore, and there were horrible squeals, very shrill and long, so long that when they stopped, when she realized that finally she wasn't hearing anything anymore, no sound at all, she didn't see her anger coming, her sudden hatred and that impulse she had to run out of the kitchen and rush to the door of the stairs, turn on the light and go through the usual routine of closing the door behind her, going down not quite facing the steps but her body turned three-quarters toward the bottom, almost sideways, slowly, her right hand on the iron banister and watching her feet, and the steps, while downstairs she didn't know yet that the dog had just bitten Woodsmoke's hand because he wanted to shut him up, he wanted to hit him on the muzzle and the dog had snapped. And then he'd beaten him up, with the dog no longer trying to bite to defend himself but to escape, to duck the blows the other was pouring on him; and the blows soon led them out through the back door. Because Woodsmoke had grabbed something blindly, a board, a tool, something heavy, he didn't know what, and he hit and kept hitting until the anger inside him bounced back with the enjoyment, the thrill, the reward at last, after such a long wait, and the animal soon inert, lying, or rather prostrate in the snow, outside, just before the woodpile.

The dog wasn't dead.

And when he left the dog outside without paying attention to him anymore, Woodsmoke didn't see the child's look up there, at the window of a bedroom, and how the child had taken a step back at the moment Woodsmoke raised his head then looked at his bloodied hand, surprised, motionless, with his hand open and his fingers spread out and motionless as well, before wiping the blood on the left sleeve of his suede jacket. He didn't see the child but the child had come back very close to the window, and the whole time before his father came into the room, he stayed like that without moving, without telling his little brother or his sister that outside, down below, near the woodpile, their old spaniel was stretched out and breathing very loudly, too loudly, almost a death-rattle, and also that there was blood on him, on his mouth, his body, the child thought he could see that from the window where he was standing, from where he'd seen the man with his hand all bloody.

But the man hadn't stayed there. He had walked into the basement. He had come back down and the child heard a noise, just as the man did, of a door opening, his mother opening the door, the cellar door.

She opened the door and she saw him—not rushing or charging or running at her or anything like that, but a quick, gray image, the smell, the man, massive, yet dark yes a dark shadow in the narrow gray passage, in the gray light from the door he'd come through. And she hardly had the time to speak when already she felt the fingers closing on her wrists; and she had the impulse to back out but that wasn't enough, the black fingernails, the bad skin, the blood, she clenches her fists, her teeth, the scream and the eyes closing, that scream wasn't enough, and she retreated to the first step, walked up a few steps like that, backwards, despite the man tightening his fingers, very hard, he's squeezing his fingers and his hands around the woman's wrists, she stammers out words, ideas, she's livid, there is terror in her eyes but not on her lips, and the blood between the fingers, dripping from Woodsmoke's right hand, dripping, that blood on her own skin too, she saw it, she almost screamed, she did not scream, did not yell or scream, nothing, she only held back her fear behind her eyes, her head, keep your head, keep it, keep everything, calm, control, think, hold on, keep back yes she kept back the screams in her throat, good, that's what you have to do, what she must do because of the children perhaps, she doesn't know at that moment why she keeps herself from screaming and trying to get loose, to get his hands off by shaking her forearms violently, no, almost nothing, she thinks of her feet that must climb up again, backwards, a few steps, she thinks, not to fall, not let him fall on me with all his weight, on me, and leave him free to touch me, to, yes suddenly the senseless images swarming up, carrying her, lifting her until she's nauseous, she thinks of the children, of the idea of rape, images she isolates, the tongue of the man, the smell of the man, his sweat and her sweat combined, their skins combined and their fear, too, both their fears and both of them now have quick sharp gestures, jerks that push their voices, their looks and her own voice which has stopped.

And she, for a moment, may have thought he was hesitating, getting hold of himself, realizing what he was doing, what he was about to commit, and her features completely contorted, her hands drawn up to her chest and the marks of his fingers on her wrists, the blood too, on her left wrist, which had stained her clothes. He saw he was bleeding a lot and he might have realized he was hurting, that the bite was hurting him, when she, too, heard—beyond his breathing so loud, both of them breathing hard, down there, at the bottom of that gray cement flight of stairs, too dark—an echo, like the muffled sound of a car door and soon footsteps, someone coming up the stairs of the entrance, his steps echoing through the house all the way to the two of them down below, in the stairway diametrically opposite the entrance, and the vibrations tell them that now it's different, something has changed, someone's here, someone's coming.

And then they looked at each other, very quickly. She, regaining her confidence but still so weak, suddenly so weak. And he, stepping back when he heard the footsteps of the one upstairs, walking up there, in the house.

Soon he would be here, in front of him.

And suddenly, looking at Chefraoui's wife, Woodsmoke smiled, yes, smiled a strange smile, a dead smile, ready now to run away, because he'd realized that perhaps for an instant, he had wanted to lay his hands on the huge bust of the woman in front of him.

And when he ran away, she didn't move; she didn't call out.

The tears came as mechanically as the breath in her chest.

It was as far from her as the trembling of her hands. It was as far from her as the marks on her wrists, as her way of opening her fingers wide, spreading them out and clenching them into a fist again so as to get the blood circulating. And she barely heard, then, the sound of the moped starting up.

That's when she thought of the children, she should get up and wash her hands, rinse out Woodsmoke's blood and the tears, which were all hers.

But she didn't move right away.

She straightened up when she heard running in the house. The time to hear the door opening and vibrations, yes, exactly, she realized someone was running down the stairs out there, outside; and it's fear that made her stand up straight, fear and nothing else.

She walked into the basement without even thinking of turning on the light. She saw the mess, the work-bench, the tools, boards, and the bikes turned over, thrown all over.

She walked toward the door of the basement and when she got there, she saw there was nobody in the yard anymore. Nothing. Only the open gate and the car. The smell of gas from the moped was floating in the air. Then she heard her husband's breath and his footsteps, and his figure soon appeared in the opening of the gate.

He walked into the yard. He looked at his wife, they didn't talk, then they went upstairs to join their children.

EVENING

So what are you going to do?

Patou's question, unasked but floating between us—sitting there, our shapes flattened by the neon light over the pool table, too white, whitening even the shadows.

Ménard looked at the mayor, then at his watch. Then I was the one he turned his eyes to. We looked at each other, but I didn't say anything. Neither did he. He looked at Patou.

The mayor sat up and looked at me with that air of being sorry, contrite, and I heard,

We have no choice.

As if I were the one who'd asked the question and not Patou, and she saying,

What d'you mean, no choice?

Finally he turned his face to her. But he didn't repeat it, he didn't say anything, and then he turned to me as if to get me to talk.

No, Patou, they have no choice.

So she shrugged, as if I wouldn't have the courage to repeat what I'd just said, or as if just by hearing myself say it I'd realize that yes, of course you can't say that, what I said is ridiculous, and, as if to anticipate what she imagined I was thinking, she wanted to insist,

What d'you mean, no choice? Rabut, he's your cousin, you have to stand up for him, he was drunk, maybe they won't press charges, they won't, Woodsmoke is what he is, he did something really stupid—

You call that stupid?

Yeah, something stupid.

It's more than stupid, Ménard said, it's way more serious than stupid.

And the other gendarme, the one who wasn't talking and drank his glass in little gulps, we saw him raise his eyes then and his double chin wiggled like the wattle of a rooster waking up,

A shock, it's a shock for everybody.

Yes, like you say, the mayor went on.

Rabut, it'd be better if you came along with us.

We talked about how it was too late now to go all the way to his place because of the snow, with the road not cleared yet; and also, we weren't sure it was such a good idea to react so fast. No, we said to ourselves, let's give it the night and we'll go up there tomorrow morning. Around eight or nine.

I looked at the time, and at that moment I regretted agreeing to meet the next morning at the church square. We'll all be there and we won't be alone, Ménard warned, we don't know what he might do, how he's going to react. The mayor didn't bat an eyelash, as if he wasn't concerned. He got up and so did the gendarmes. As for me I sat there a few seconds more, taking time to think of this suddenly aggressive sentence that I didn't say—it was there in my mouth and I didn't understand why that sentence came to me when the three of them got up, that particular sentence, those words I swallowed back, but in my mind they struck home:

Mayor, do you remember the first time you saw an Arab?

But of that, I said nothing. I didn't even catch myself looking at the mayor to check what I already knew, his age, yes, how old was he, in those years? Did he go there, did he see, was it the first time he was leaving home, leaving his old family cocoon, did he leave behind a family, a fiancée, for months and months? Was he afraid, was he bored, did he hold a rifle and get to know the damp, sweaty feel of it in his hands and the stifling heat, and yes—I know all that.

I know he's a little too young.

Patou looked at the gendarmes and the mayor, staring at them with a kind of intransigence and lassitude, as the mayor took out his wallet and she said the round was on her. Then in the same tone, this time in a gentle voice almost,

Maybe they won't press charges?

They will, believe me. I sent a doctor for the wife. The children are traumatized and she's traumatized too, we can't just let things like this happen.

Ménard spoke very serenely, very calmly. But it was final, and of course Patou didn't answer right away. She walked behind her bar, and without looking at Ménard or the mayor, she went to get a cigarette, lit it, and sat down next to her husband by the cash register. I ended up going over to them. Ménard put his hand on the doorknob. He waited before opening the door.

Sure, I know you can't do that. I know it's unacceptable, Patou said. I was sure he'd do something dumb someday. It could've been worse. I mean—

I know what you mean, Ménard interrupted, but don't think I'm just going to let it go.

And it was only at that moment that the mayor looked really interested or concerned, at the moment they were about to leave;

that's when he came out with—just like that, almost casually, or rather, no, let's say with a knowing look—between ourselves, we'd agree, no question, it's kind of obvious, see, the alcoholics, the drunks, pains in the ass, parasites, the ones we have to put up with, and who pays for that, us, the taxpayer and all that, you understand; a little shrug, we don't have too many bums around here, or beggars, and that's good, the mayor seemed to imply, and then he said okay, we know how it is, right? Sure we do. And Patou looked at him without batting an eyelash, impassive, except that she got up to put out her cigarette and let him say— without telling him to bug off or even making the effort to look at him—that the whole thing was premeditated, that business with the brooch, he was provoking them, pure provocation, just theatrics, right, otherwise it's impossible, he's not that stupid, or crazy, or ignorant, not so out of it he couldn't realize what a scandal there'd be, and honestly, to go buy a jewel like that, he's twisted, nuts, but still, frankly, is that whole story true?

Rabut, answer, is it true, can you confirm it? I mean, you're still confirming it?

And me raising my hands to assent again for the umpteenth time, it's true, when Patou didn't sit back down but stood up very straight to say,

No, it's not true.

And she explained she was with him just before it happened, and also that both of them, Jean-Marc and she (and her quick gesture of turning to her husband to ask for his approval, which came immediately, with a nod and a yes, almost shouted, dispro- portionately), the two of them had known it for weeks even, for weeks Woodsmoke had been planning what he was going to do, not premeditating or plotting, no, the only thing he premeditated was to give a woman who's a widow, can't you understand that, give her a present the way men do, like you all do, for your wives. Yeah, I know, you're going to tell me she's his sister not his wife. But that's exactly what he'd been thinking about for a long time, that's what he premeditated, see. He told himself she has nobody to give her that kind of present. A jewel. But *he* thought of it! He'd thought of it and I think it was really good of him, don't you think, to think of his sister, telling himself nobody else would give her a jewel like that because she didn't have anybody to do it?

Then the mayor and the gendarmes left. Without really answering her, with a gesture of their heads that meant they understood, or maybe didn't, and didn't know what to think. Or just to thank her for the wine and say good-bye.

I wanted to say something about going back to the community hall, but the three men had barely left when Patou said we should defend him because he'd acted like a madman, someone who's desperate, insane, a stupid drunk, true, silent and angry, sure, whatever, however you want to look at it, but not wicked. He's not mean, she repeated again and again when I looked at her and looked at her husband, too, his eyes intently watching his wife's hands when she put out her cigarette; the cigarette she'd hardly smoked, broken in half with a sharp tap—her fingernails thick red, shiny, vermilion, and the ashes and the whiteness of the cigarette paper, her lipstick on the yellow butt, and me looking at her the way her husband was looking at her, too. I could still hear myself with that sentence rolling inside my mouth,

Mayor, you remember the first time you saw an Arab? You remember? Do you remember? Is it possible to remember? Does anyone? Is it possible to remember that?

I could still hear that sentence and already, at that moment, I felt a whole part of myself collapse inside of me, sinking, crashing, a part that had only been hidden or tucked away, I don't know, or asleep, and this time that old carcass asleep in my head had awakened with a kind of jerk, eyes wide open, anxious, with a heavy head, when I wondered why that sentence had surged up and jumped so hard in my chest—because that movement of the heart felt like the anxiety of waiting, waiting for another appointment, like the day of an exam, and that anger, too, and also that scandal inside me, of wanting to silence the gendarmes and Ménard with his descriptions and his details, with me making it worse when I'd heard his words, inventing them, inviting the faces, the fears, the images, everything he'd said, and also that movement, my reversal, why I wanted to defend Woodsmoke by throwing these words in the mayor's face,

Mayor, do you remember?

And the violent shame I felt at that sentence, at the way it popped up. The shame that had pressed so hard that the words did not come out, could not, and instead of that aggression they wanted to direct at the mayor and the gendarmes, they had given way to astonishment, to stupor at hearing in my head words that had come out of nowhere, and so clearly, so absolutely pronounced, not fragments of ideas, images, or confusion, but that plain and simple sentence, and behind it the certainty, the irritation I was surprised to feel myself, like a wave, a surge, an attack to say enough, that's enough, and thus defend something in Woodsmoke that had nothing to do with family ties, that wasn't friendship, respect, or even a kind of compassion or the need to defend someone, with no justification other than that surge of feeling for someone who's wrong and who you know nobody's going to defend.

I'm saying that, but it was very confused. I remember it now, because I recall that those ideas were troubling me as I looked at Patou.

And instead of answering her, instead of saying something, I stayed there in front of her, looking at the cigarette broken in half in the bright black ashtray, with that vermilion red too, Marlboro, the same red as Patou's fingernails.

Want another one?

No, I'm leaving.

I walked to the door, grabbed the doorknob. Then I turned around. I came back to the bar and I'm the one who launched the attack, without warning, in a voice that was too shrill, its tone breaking by itself, the time to clear my throat, cough, and hide behind my clenched fist when I said,

No, Patou, Woodsmoke was always a weird guy, you don't know him like I do. See, I'm not sure you get it. I can tell you lots of things about him, about his life, when he was young, his marriage, childhood, yes, that's right, his childhood, we can start with that if you want. And not just details like torturing animals or silly things kids do that don't mean a thing, cutting off lizards' tails, weighing down frogs and tossing them into the water, watching them drown, making them smoke so they explode, shooting birds and hens with a buckshot rifle—the games country kids play—I'm not talking about that.

I mean after that, later, when he was a teenager.

You know the story of his sister, the death of his sister Reine, that won't tell you anything, but if I can look at Woodsmoke without thinking about that, it's been, what, only a few years, because before, I couldn't; every time I would see him again the way he was back there against the wall of the bedroom, with the whitewashed walls, the candles, and the very low cot where she was stretched out, dying, bloodless, with the old women from La Migne sniveling away, the stale odor and the smell of paraffin and cologne, and the missal on the little table, the damp wash-cloth on her forehead, and the smell of dust, the pollen flying outside and the silence, the crucifix over the bed, the lace doilies on the furniture, the rosaries, the hugs and kisses, the wailing you have no idea how sickening it all was, you feel like slapping someone, not one single new house yet but decrepit old stone houses, crooked, small, thick, dark, cluttered, tightly closed, like clumsy hands jealous of their little secrets. And it stank in there, I remember so well those odors of stagnant water, of soap, dirty dishes, the buzzing of flies against the windowpane, the oilcloth with wine stains on it, I remember him, too, in his corner of the room near the window, with his back against the wall, his look of disgust, so stiff, upright as the image of virtue or justice or whatever, when he was looking at his dying sister and the crib next to her.

Let me explain. Yes, I'm going too fast.

The little sister died leaving behind a child with no father or mother, nothing but a body and the wonder of being in the world, his astonishment and the astonishment of the others, all the others, the whole family, the Old Lady caring for the child, while the others will only have words of disapproval, whispers, and snigger for the next thirty or forty years to get over it, over that, but also over Bernard — he wasn't Woodsmoke at the time. With his neck leaning forward rigidly, he was playing with the blade of a penknife, cleaning his fingernails, not looking around him when the others were crying or looking tenderly at the baby, just looking at his nails and the black dirt on the point of the blade, mumbling rubbish. I swear, I repeated to Patou and Jean-Marc, he's not as nice as you seem to say, or think, he's not just some poor guy busted up by life, no, not just that, even if life busted him up, but his stubbornness, the hardness in his eyes when he was there the day his little sister died, a teenager, don't think I'm making it up, I'm not, and also I remember her very well, brown hair, pretty, shy, dead not long after she'd given birth, dead from shame, rage, pain as well, when she heard her brother's silence through her fatigue and loss of blood, her brother standing upright against the whitewashed wall, his implacable, cold stare, articulating very clearly, very slowly and without anger, almost in a hushed voice, saying she was a slut, I remember when I came into the room, slut he was saying, whispering, repeating, coldly, slut, they had to make him leave because he'd shrugged, you can't forget that, you know, I can't forgive things like that, because he was brutal, calm, and determined.

I mean really, I'm not talking about the kittens he used to throw against the wall when they were born, just to see, I'm not talking about us boys in the back country, our stupidity, our mindlessness. In those days we hadn't seen much and we didn't expect anything—because at fourteen, you'd go work in the fields and dream of getting a driver's license and taking the girl next door to the dance on Saturday nights, to the fair, the merry-go-round on Sundays and Easter Monday, and that was about it.

And then that silence when I stopped talking. My exhaustion. Jean-Marc walked over and poured a cognac that he put on the bar. I picked it up right away, but I didn't drink. I looked at the glass for a long time, and at the little amber-colored puddle inside.

And I went on.

Sure, sure you like him because he pulled on your heartstrings. He told you about Paris, his years there, and you liked that, a local guy who knew where you were from. Not only the Eiffel Tower and all, but the streets and the avenues. A country boy capable of bowling you over with stories we had no clue about, which made you laugh, the twenty-first arrondissement when everybody knows Paris has only twenty, and bits for insiders that he would repeat, repeat to us, repeat to me too, with his underhand way of looking down on us, people from here. You thought that was great, okay, I can understand. A local guy who knew where you guys came from, what it meant to live on the outskirts of Paris, who knew it meant long rides on the metro to get to work, and Billancourt, where the factory was. Maybe it's because of all that, but let me tell you: I never saw him there, in his worker's life, in his overalls, on the assembly line at Renault. What I saw is when he came back.

I could talk about him for hours, about his body becoming thicker and thicker, hanging around town to see this one and that one again, and not just his old buddies, not just the Fabre brothers and their goats who used to walk in the fields all the goddamn day, not just the guys from his childhood, from La Migne or the villages nearby, the neighbors—what was left of the neighbors, the ones who hadn't gotten rid of the farm but left their folks behind to finish a story as old as the stones, astonished that their sons had gotten the hell out. No, he was really surprised, almost shocked, when he came back, to see he wasn't the only one who'd left home, expecting to find the sons in place of their fathers and the daughters in place of their mothers. Except that in the meantime, well okay, fine, I'm not going to rehash it again, you know, we all know, the new houses, how they grew where the factories used to be, Solange's house was one of the first, one of the biggest, in a field.

Rabut.

Before, there was nothing here. La Bassée—it was only fields and even seashells from I don't know how far back.

Rabut.

And so, when he came back, after all those years, for him it wasn't just the surprise of finding a completely different, drastically changed world, but something else, yes, something shocking, I'm sure, he'd thought he was strong or smart because he'd managed to leave — actually no, let me correct that, not to leave. To not come back, I should say. Because as far as leaving goes, well, nobody asked his opinion.

Rabut.

It's more that after his stay at Club Algeria, yeah, that's right, always a joke for you, that's the way it was with us already, kidding around all the time, he had dared not to come back and go his own sweet way, his stubborn old way and today just look at him —

Rabut.

Rabut. Why are you saying all that. No point piling up on him. He doesn't need that. Right? Don't you think?

I didn't answer Jean-Marc.

I raised my glass of cognac and put it to my lips. The smell came stroking my nostrils and warmed me up, but I didn't drink. I set the glass down again and followed Patou with my eyes; she'd gone over to the other side of the bar and without saying anything, started picking up the chairs and putting them upside down on the tables. Jean-Marc's the one who spoke.

He said: Listen, Rabut, your cousin is what he is, but when he talks about you, he doesn't say anything bad. He says the graduate and that makes him laugh all by himself, but that's all. And then sometimes, okay, it's true, when he's really drunk and lays it on thick cursing the Arabs and the whole world, but still, what's gonna happen, they'll give him a lecture, they'll throw him in the slammer, and then what, what does that change, he's got to be half gone already barging into people's houses like that, I don't get it, he lost his head and tomorrow, tomorrow maybe it'll be too late, maybe, I mean—

He stopped talking all of a sudden, leaving his sentence hanging and his eyes on the glass door: Nicole was on the other side and was hesitating whether to come in.

She looked tiny in her coat, and seemed surprised, worried, almost angry to see me here, at the bar, with this cognac I couldn't bring myself to drink, looking at its amber color while Jean-Marc was talking, as if to find shelter in it, a place to settle my wandering ideas. And then I had to interrupt Nicole when she began asking me questions,

What did the gendarmes want?

What did they want with the mayor?

What did they want that you couldn't say in front of us?

What's going on?

And her eyes seeking an answer from Jean-Marc and Patou. But Patou not reacting, saying nothing and barely raising her eyes. She kept on putting the chairs on top of the tables and then went to get a broom.

And so okay, I told Nicole.

What about Solange. We have to tell Solange. We have to. And call Saïd to see how they're doing. His wife, and the main thing is, if he didn't hurt the children—Nicole's worried voice, her eyes almost panic-stricken before I told her that as far as that goes, everything was fine.

They saw the doctor and I don't know what's going to happen, they don't want to press charges but the mayor is insisting
and the police, too. They're pressuring them to do it, they want
to see them tomorrow for Chefraoui to press charges, for him
to do it, not to be scared, that's what they say, that he's scared.

They also want me to go to Woodsmoke's with them tomorrow morning. They want to hear him and tell him they're not
letting it drop.

And I couldn't go on because at that moment, I don't know
why that sentence came back like that, it flashed through my
mind, a dazzling attack. I shook it off by emptying my glass of
cognac in one gulp, saying to Patou and Jean-Marc in an exag-
geratedly loud voice,

Okay, I'll keep you posted,

And to Nicole,

Come on, let's go,

When I was saying to myself,

What is this, Rabut, what's wrong with you, what's this uneasy
feeling, when you wouldn't forgive Woodsmoke for anything in
the world, what is it, why is there something else under the hatred
and scorn and that old resentment against him that never went
away, why is there something else, why do you feel something
else, another emotion, further away, underground and rising
and whispering unhealthy words to you like fear, this anger too,
no, it's not anger, it's what, what is it, what is that thing, that
sentence that keeps coming back.

Mayor, Mayor, you remember the first time you saw an Arab?
Mayor, you remember? Do you remember? Is it possible to
remember? Does anyone?

Is it possible to remember that?

What, what are you saying?

Does anyone?

What are you saying?

Nothing.

And at that moment, what I remembered—it was not a memory exactly, not yet, but an image in front of me, almost as true and real as the cold and the snow: on a spring morning at the supermarket—the spring of seventy-seven or seventy-eight— people stopped shopping, dumfounded, astonished at the mere sight, so close to them, of a couple whose extraordinariness consisted in a djellaba the color of anise and a light blue scarf, and hennaed hands.

Nothing else.

It was the first time we were seeing foreigners here. And what we hadn't imagined was that little minute of astonishment all of them felt—our wives, relatives, friends, who all those years ago had waited for us for months, read our letters, seen our snapshots, and wondered what they *really* looked like, on the other side of the sea.

Yes, the first days, the first months, that strange discovery and curiosity.

And then, for us, it was like seeing the dead again or ghosts the way they come back sometimes, at night, even if we don't talk about it, we know, of course, all of us, from seeing the other guys, the Algeria vets and their way of not talking about that, that and all the rest. We talked about this and that, about the annual drawing, the lottery to organize, the next banquet, the next *méchoui*.

But not a word about Chefraoui when he landed here with his whole family, not even to ask ourselves where he was from, was he Kabyle or what, nothing, we didn't ask. We could have. And even talked with him, we could have said,

Oh yes, I know that area, it's nice around there.

But no. Not that either. We didn't do it.

Except that we thought about it, we did, but like a thought to be ashamed of, that we were ashamed of, like seeing a part of ourselves surge up again, the old story of our youth.

But everybody must have had slightly unhealthy thoughts, secretly, that he kept to himself, thinking he was the only one who'd ruminated on them for years, all alone, buried deep in the folds of his memories, in the corners, the shadows, swamps, still waters, or just between friends when you're a little drunk,

Hey, did you see the Algerian guy, he's our age, yes, same age as us.

Except.

You know where he's from, where he comes from?

And even at the start we weren't sure he was Algerian, he could have been Moroccan or Tunisian. But for us, of course he was Algerian.

The cold, when Nicole and I went out. The cold, when we crossed the street, almost running. We walked quickly into the community center where the light, so white, so cold too, the silence and that big room almost empty now greeted us, and we left all those ideas, pictures, and memories at the door, but with our hearts beating just a little faster and a name and a face: Solange.

The tablecloths were gone from the tables, which were no more than wooden boards now, except for the one in the middle where the last guests had gathered. So it was like we were in a very small

circle now, almost closed around Solange. But that didn't last
long. The time for her to understand, to repress her urge to cry
and let anger invade her, when she just said we'd finish all this
food the next day, whoever wanted to come, they could—her
way of asking people to leave, to cut short all those discussions;
she knew what they'd be about, or rather, about whom.

And she did not want that.

Didn't want Woodsmoke to be blamed for all the lingering
hatred and resentments in the family, in life, here, everywhere,
because this time she wouldn't be able to defend him. And she
wouldn't even try. But in fact there was no way she could not give
in, not go in that old direction they'd always wanted to impose on
her since childhood, because everybody was already blaming her
brother, this particular brother, for being a kind of invisible child,
for the sneaky, hateful way he had of hiding in the Cheval Blanc
woods or in the corn and wheat fields, where he would disappear
for days on end with his Fabre buddies, kids as dirty and dumb
as the goats that led them around, yes, the goats decided what
road to take, and with their cheeks burned by the sun or their
lips split open by the cold or whatever, the boys would follow
them, whistling, along the roadside and into people's fields that
the goats devastated, calmly, indifferently, ripping up seedlings
and shoots. With the Old Lady and Father both angry, always,
like everyone else, forever angry, at him.

As if he had to bear all the anger of the others and never talk
back, ever.

And he didn't talk back, ever.

No way. No way she'd go along with the others, all the others
who were just waiting for that, to bring him down once and for
all. And it's because she loved him that she remained speechless,
with her face so pale; and it's also because they knew she couldn't

stand hearing them put him down that they all got up and left to get their coats, one after the other, walking unobtrusively to the door with a quick thank you and disappearing almost without a word.

And yet that didn't stop me from talking, suddenly blurting out words that had been reined in for too long, without anyone answering, only surprised to find myself talking so loud and having to dig up things so far in the past to launch my attack, from the time Bernard, not yet Woodsmoke, had surfaced again.

I walked away from the table and went over to stand against the radiator, with my hands behind my back to warm them up. While I talked, the table was being cleared. I watched Nicole clearing it off and saying nothing, Solange walking by as if she were only paying attention to the glasses in her hands, to the cups and pitchers of water she was bringing back to the kitchen on the other side, walking in front of me and staring straight in front of her, without really listening to what I was saying, when I felt I couldn't stop that flood anymore—

Remember, Solange. Nicole, you remember. Do both of you remember? All three of us remember, we all do, he came back after fifteen years, a little more, even—

In seventy-six.

How come you remember?

The heat.

Yes, seventy-six maybe, I answered Solange, who'd spoken without looking at me, without waiting for anything, back some-where inside herself, since Chefraoui wasn't living here yet, a little earlier then, in seventy-five, seventy-six.

Yes, that's it. We had to go pick him up at the station and I was the one who got stuck with it, none of his brothers wanted to—I can still see myself in my Citroën with the bags of cement in back because I was finishing making slabs for the flowerbeds and when he got into the car with his stuff, an old wooden suitcase and a big plastic bag with heavy sweaters that couldn't fit in the suitcase rolled up inside it, I remember he hardly said hello, as if we had just seen each other the night before.

You here for a long time?

Merely glancing at the back of the car, surprised to see the bags of cement, before mumbling,

Dunno. Maybe. Probably.

And then, nothing. Silence. After fifteen years. And I hesitate, wait, try again,

And, Mireille?

The only answer was the engine of the Citroën.

And already he seemed harder than he used to be, as soon as he got back I said to myself something's wrong, broken, his eyes are too blue, almost transparent, empty, same mustache his father had, and that surly look old people have around here.

You remember how he was right after he got back, how he never answered anything, and even about Mireille, why he left her like that, his wife and his two children too, the two kids, nothing, not a word about his kids, not even to you, Solange, even to you he said nothing about that, about his kids, he left, he abandoned his kids and he never said a thing. That same arrogance, too, behind the wrinkles and his very white, very dry skin. His hair combed back, long and greasy, hanging down to his neck. And then a vague smell of sweat like when you sleep in your clothes.

I told myself he must've left home a few days earlier, maybe, and he'd hesitated for a long time before deciding to show up here, to face the people here and his past again: his mother, that is.

I know Solange wasn't listening. She was thinking about what she wanted to do, what she thought she should do.

Which was to go home and call Chefraoui.

And so we went with her. We got to her house barely twenty minutes later, Nicole and I sitting in the kitchen, listening to Solange's voice coming from the hallway.

We could see her from behind, we watched her standing there, stooped, the back of her neck leaning forward over the telephone, her hand clutching it tightly. We thought we had to watch her intently, support her, be there for her when she turned to us for help, as if we could hear what Chefraoui was telling her, even if she had withdrawn into herself a little at the start of the conversation, to summon up the courage to dial the number and hear the phone ring—it had rung for a long time, we were already sitting in the kitchen and I can see myself pouring glasses of water for Nicole three or four times, and the plastic bottle that was too thin and almost sank in under the pressure of my fingers, Solange's voice, her gaze, and her way of turning to us, wide-eyed, her voice trembling when she had to speak,

Yes. Yes, can you give me your daddy, please?

Yes, Saïd, it's Solange.

How are things? The children, your wife, tell me, how are you—

You sure? Really—

The gendarmes and the mayor came, they told my cousin the whole thing. They're saying—

Yes, Saïd, I know. Saïd, I'm so—

Your wife and your children . . . your children were scared? Who's the one who answered the phone? And your wife, what can we do, you sure everything's going to be all right? Really? I don't get it. What got into him, I don't get it, I don't know what goes through his head, I'm really, you know, I, I just wanted—

No, no, Saïd. I don't know, Saïd. I—

They said they'd go see him tomorrow morning anyway and I decided to go with them, with Rabut too, we'll go, he's got to say something, he's got to apologize; no, I can't let that go, no way, he may be my brother but this is unacceptable, no, I don't want to, I can't, you understand, it's not normal—

Saïd, I *know* you don't want to make trouble, you're not the one making trouble—

That's nice Saïd, but look, honestly, yes, your children, tell me, they're okay, he didn't touch them, it's true, you'd tell me, right, you would, yes—

Your wife. Yes. She's crying. Now she's crying. I.

I really don't know what to say. No, he's the one who's making trouble not you and I don't see why—

No, no, no.

No.

Saïd.

Yes okay, if you want, but *I* want him to apologize and go over and see you and your wife, he has to—

Yes, I know.

The police and the mayor want you to press charges. They'll come back to try to convince you and I . . . frankly, I can't tell you not to do it, I can't, I feel sorry for Bernard, but I can't.

And then there was a long silence.

A long moment while she hesitated before hanging up. Then the long, painful time it took her to walk back to us and stand there looking at us, not having the courage to say a word, or make a move either—Solange, who could never stay put and was never seen to sit down except the better to stand up, tidy up, move things around, turn on the TV and turn up the volume, change the channel. But now, she didn't turn on the TV. She kept standing in front of us without saying anything, with her arms hanging, and then she started shaking her head as if to say no, as if she were saying no to herself, as if something inside herself wanted to say no, and finally she was able to say, softly at first, with no other movement but a breath pushed out of her lips, no, as if she had succeeded in unfolding a narrow space in her skin, so thin and tiny it was hardly perceptible.

I remember, she said, I remember, at the beginning, when Saïd arrived here, when we worked together, at first people didn't say anything, everything was fine, and then one day we had to vote, elect the representatives of the town hall staff, or union delegates or whatever, I don't remember. I know nobody wanted to run. We were at the town hall. At a meeting. We were all there. We all know each other and nobody wanted to run because everybody knows being a delegate is time-consuming, and you have to take the job seriously; I remember what happened when Saïd volunteered. What happened between the people, that moment of, I don't know what to call it, embarrassment, silence, something going on between the people, in their eyes or I don't know, no, something in the air, and it was that fat guy, Bouboule, with his kid's smile and his chubby face with little creases around the eyes and under his chin, who said what the others were thinking and nobody could admit and accept, as if, yes, we didn't realize what was happening.

Her voice, Solange's voice, when she was saying they hadn't wanted Chefraoui as their representative.

And he had protested a little, but not for long, and she saw him getting upset, sort of, expressing how unhappy he was about it, but his surprise mainly, saying, repeating, less and less loudly, less and less sure of himself, as if he ended up by wondering if in fact he wasn't the one responsible for the silence and the embarrassment, as if doubt could slip in, as if being so close to us he himself could start thinking the same way as the people here, to the point of admitting that it wasn't right for him to run for that position, to represent us here, and useless, almost wrong, tactless, to say that he worked here like everybody else, that he was like everybody else, that he paid his taxes like we all did.

He had hesitated. And then he had stopped talking altogether. We listened to the silence, only disturbed by the typewriter of the secretary at the reception desk.

The three of us just stayed like that, and of course between us there was the image of Chefraoui and Woodsmoke, and soon between the two of them the image of the brooch in its deep blue box.

What did you do with the brooch?

It's on the dining room table.

Solange answered Nicole without really looking at her, exhausted by the phone call and Chefraoui's voice, exhausted by the whole day and also by the effort to understand, to figure out how to react. That's when she talked about going to the jewelers to find out how Bernard had paid; and that's when the others came up, the family, and she had to admit that they'd been right not to hide their anger. That's what, suddenly, Solange couldn't stop herself from saying. How, in fact, with the brooch he had completely taken on the contempt he'd always felt for them all his life, as she knew and never wanted to admit, since they used to tell her, they always told her,

Right, Rabut? You always said that, didn't you.

Yeah, I did, it's true, I did say it, I told you what your brother's really like, you know very well what he's like.

And I thought, what can I say—what more can I say, really—when he came back here and settled into our great-uncle's house up there, how shocked I was too, yes, shocked, to see among the few framed snapshots on the walls, instead of pictures of his children, just shots of the little girl he used to play with back in Algeria—God, it's all coming back, I'm thinking back to the little girl with her hair in a bun and her Arabic name I've forgotten, her slippers and cape buttoned all the way up the neck, and those pictures where you see her looking serious, concentrating, in one of them she's looking at the camera, right in the middle of the picture in front of the window of a house (you can see a rather thick flowerbed and the scaly wall, the curtain inside, the window open, her on the little scooter with her face turned slightly to her right, where her shadow covers the gravel. I remember the spot very well, the rudimentary scooter, the serious, shy little girl), and that photo was there along with a few others. But that one had been enlarged, and another one too, with the same little girl on her scooter: but this time she's in motion, she's in profile with her face lowered, and Bernard is holding the kid's shoulders, you see one hand and the other is invisible, on the other side. He's wearing an army cap and he's concentrating on helping the child. I remember that building in back very well and also the side of the hill and the brush, the white sky, the cement path they're on, and my shadow all the way at the bottom of the picture, my head, my hands, and the camera forming one single shape, like a crawling animal.

The old yellow, scalloped snapshots with that wide border, and not one single picture of his own children. That's what shocked me. Not one picture of his wife or his children either, although he had some of his friends from Algeria, the one where he's with Idir. You can see both of them in the picture—that one wasn't enlarged—a little steel-gray frame where Idir is posing with Bernard on a town square, with all the blue-white-and-red flags in the white sky of the Oran countryside . . . yes, shocked to see that Bernard had dared to frame those photos and then put them up on the wall when he didn't have a single one of his wife and children—of his wife, well okay, but his children, how is it possible to reach the point where you feel contempt for your own children and want to forget them? Did he talk about his children, say one word about them? No, of course not. He turned up here one day without telling anybody or even deigning to explain why he'd left Paris, why he'd abandoned his wife and children, a man capable of doing that, of doing something much worse—but that, we can't talk about, because the words we had to say, the words we'd have to say, that we would've had to say, maybe, if—well, no, forget it—pictures, memories—there weren't any words for that, both of us knew it, Bernard and I, when he came back here over fifteen years ago, when I saw his photos from Algeria in our great-uncle's house.

And yet he dared to frame them, hang them on the wall, show them there, and not say a word about them, say nothing, as if they were vacation pictures, say nothing about them to me, to me, who he'd seen so often over there and shared the—okay, let's say, dared think that years later both of us can meet, and he's left those photos—on the walls between us—and says nothing about them, photos that watch us stay silent, me, who could have asked, casually,

You still have nightmares?

When I didn't ask anything, just because I'd realized there was no picture of his children, no recent picture, just, in frames, images and places I knew: some of the snapshots I'd taken myself, and there were people I had known over there, too. Idir in uniform posing proudly on the square with blue-white-and-red flags on Bastille Day, and he'd soon be dead in the same exact spot, without the blue-white-and-red flags behind him.

Not one shot of his children.

And I hadn't even dared say to him, when we'd found a mattress for him, and sheets, blankets, some furniture, and that big old pot, too; I hadn't even dared ask him anything, not even,

Why're you coming back?

How come you're not saying anything about your kids?

And your wife? I met your wife the same time you did, back there, in Oran. You could tell me what became of her, Mireille.

But I know he wouldn't have answered.

He's here, calm and composed, fixing up the great-uncle's house any way he can, looking for cement to shore up the walls and ceiling; the whole roof is in danger of collapsing. He wants to settle here, in this godforsaken spot, so far from everything except his mother's house and La Migne. And of that, not a word, either. He works every day at fixing up his house and very soon you can see him prowling around his mother's house, trying to go over to her place, waiting, looking, watching for the moment she'll agree to talk to him. We also know that soon she'll almost be afraid of him, and she'll claim she hears him walking around her house at night.

But she always refused to talk to him.

And you, Solange, that's why you began to protect him and help him. And you wouldn't listen when you were told he was completely crazy and had started drinking; some people even claimed they saw him in the forest at night with his rifle (and you, you would answer them adamantly,

What about them, what the hell were they doing in the forest at night?)

And also whole days and evenings clinging to the counter of the bar, staggering, chewing tobacco, rolling a ball of spit under his mustache, boasting, too, of killing Arabs, of getting rid of the Arabs once and for all, liberating us, he said, from the Arabs; and he'd even talked about Chefraoui when he moved here, claiming he would get rid of him for us, too.

That's the way Bernard talked. When he became Woodsmoke.

We all pretended not to hear. All of us pretended to believe he was just talking like drunks talk, eaten away by alcohol as much as by resentment and hatred. But with him you could also feel the bitterness of a pretentious man forced to give up all his pretentions, which were falling one after the other like masks that couldn't stay attached to his face.

But dangerous, no. We didn't think he was dangerous. But anyway, the others thought he was.

As for me, I told myself, I suspected, at least I think I suspected, I think I interpreted some of his gestures as signs of violence, not just the violence Février had told me about, years after we got back here, the day he came to see me, me and a few buddies.

And so, what happened today—

Rabut. When he came back the Old Lady didn't even want to see him.

Yes, Solange, I know.

Her own son, who she hadn't seen for fifteen years.

I know. He got married, you're the only one he told.

She could've forgiven him. She should've. A son is a son. I tell myself, if one of my sons. It seems to me that for a mother, a son, I think. Nicole.

Yeah.

Yes, that's what counts and even the Old Lady, even her, she was unhappy about that. When Father died, he didn't come down for the funeral. Honestly Rabut, how'd you expect her to forgive that? He never did introduce his wife and children to us, his own family, you realize that?

Okay, Solange, but still, he came back. He settled down here because he wanted to see his mother and come back, start over, here. And then, maybe—

What are you thinking, Rabut, it's over. It's all over—

No, Solange, not over. I remember when he came back as if it was yesterday and the more time goes by, the older it is, the clearer it gets even: not a word, to anybody. He just fixed up the great-uncle's house.

And I remember, in the barn—you remember the barn, don't you, Solange, of course you do, your wedding banquet, the place where we all used to leave old things, bikes, mopeds, even my father's old Citroën is still there; Bernard could have wanted to empty it out, get rid of it all, but no, no, not a chance, as if he'd come back to start over just where he'd left off fifteen years earlier, when he was forced to drop everything here, especially his money, that damned money that made him totally crazy, Février used to say so—Nicole, you remember Février, don't you? That, too, was a long time ago, he came at the end of the sixties and we haven't seen him since—yes, his cash and his mother, that's all he talked about when he got to Algeria, not even that they put a uniform on his back, or the hours on the train, or the transit barracks, the sea, the boat, the two of us only twenty kilometers apart, both of us on the coast, with me in the city and he, with Février, in a quiet post guarding a forest of gas or oil tanks, I don't remember which, at the foot of the hills, as if he couldn't see anything but the money he'd won in the lottery, because he was obsessed by it, the fat bundle of money he had to leave in his mother's hands: he was sure she'd find a way to spend it. He was outraged. He was already totally mad in those days, just like when he was a kid, so serious about church, taking everything too seriously, rigid, unable to bend his principles a little—

Rabut, that's not true.

Yes it is true, Solange. It's true, I remember, I do, I saw him, and even Mireille could tell you, because the first time we got together again it was in Oran, I remember, the bar, Mireille, Gisèle, Philibert, and the other people too. I remember the people and everything, what Mireille looked like when we met her.

What are you talking about? What does that have to do with anything? Nothing.

Yes it does.

No it doesn't, he wasn't like that before. A man who hasn't had a woman for such a long time, you don't know what it's like, you talk, you talk, but that, you can't understand—

Solange, I'm not saying we understand loneliness—

No, Rabut, good thing you're not saying that.

I know, Solange, I do.

No, you don't.

Then Nicole walked out of the kitchen. She went to the dining room and came back without saying anything, holding the deep blue box in her hands without even daring to look at it. A silence, just the time for Solange to notice what I was staring at in Nicole's hands. And it was Nicole who asked,

Février—did you ever tell me about him?

He came to see us once, just once, a long time ago, years ago, at the house. He went on and on about his part of the country. A tall guy with glasses.

Maybe, it was a long time ago. Is it because of him you ended up—

Yeah, me. For Bernard and him, it was a lot worse.

And then that silence again. Lower my eyes, maybe. Or smile. Or pour myself another glass of water.

Let me see.

Nicole held out the deep blue box to me. I opened it and looked at the brooch. Yes, a fine piece of jewelry. I took it out of its box and nobody said anything, their eyes fixed on the brooch and also on the box where I put the jewel back, without saying anything, letting the whiteness of the neon vibrate over our heads along with the fridge behind us.

But then Solange spoke up, softly, while her hand took back the box and held it delicately, without opening it, but without taking her eyes off it, without looking at me or raising her eyes, only asking,

But what if Saïd presses charges?

She asked that without really asking, more like a thought, a stage in the fear that was beginning to rise in her and was soon going to overwhelm her, take her over, I was sure of it already. And in fact, that's why I still didn't dare leave, even though I really wanted to get back home. And Nicole's insistent look. That look also asking to cut this moment short because we quickly knew what it would hold, how it would expand once the night had moved forward, deepened, even more silent under the snow; that night, which would be waiting for us at home, too. A night we'd really rather put off a while longer, the time to accept some herb tea, yes, warm our hands by squeezing a cup of tea, feel the warmth and the sweet smell of verbena or mint.

Maybe you're hungry?

No.

I can take out some pizza if you want?

No, herb tea'll be fine.

Above all not to be alone, each of us with our own questions and memories, the time to make ourselves believe that between the three of us we would find a solution with words alone when words were hardly enough to cover the electric vibration of the neon and the water boiling in the saucepan, the sound of the fridge, a car already far off on Avenue Mitterand and dogs barking after it, when Solange looked at me almost nastily, letting the resentment that had always festered inside her explode,

Listen, Rabut. Rabut?

What?

What did Bernard ever do to you, to make all of you hate him so much your whole lives? You know why, at least?

Nothing.

You don't know?

No, he never did anything.

Does anybody know that, can anybody tell me, why you and the others—all the others, why you never could stand him, why you never could look him in the face? Especially my mother. The Old Lady, oh yeah, the Old Lady, for her Bernard was the absolute worst—Rabut, you remember how she used to look at him? She never could stand him. She chose not to love him just the way she chose to love this one or that one, the way she loved the others, some more some less, with differences, preferences, sure, but like in all families, except that her son, what she used to say about him, badmouthing him all the time like that, she had no problem calling him a thief and a good-for-nothing in front of people we hardly knew. And even to his face, staring at him, provoking him, just waiting for him to answer back so she'd have the excuse she needed to justify herself.

Solange was quiet for a few seconds, then looked at me intently.

Even Papa didn't like him that much. Even Papa, nice as he was, he never stood up for him—I, I just don't get it.

I mean, I don't understand what he did, for all of you to treat him like that, never trusting him. He wasn't my worst brother. Far from it. That's what I can't understand. It's just that from the time he was very young he knew how to fight and he liked to fight, it's true, that's true, yes, and lecture people too maybe, maybe he had a big mouth like you say, but that's all, really—

No. No, Solange, that's not all. Don't you remember your sister? And him cleaning his fingernails with his knife while she was in her bed dying? Don't you remember what he was saying there, how she was a slut and it served her right and —

No Rabut. Rabut, stop it.

And Solange getting up abruptly, leaving the water boiling in the saucepan without paying attention to it; Nicole went to turn it off before pouring us the tea — Solange walking quickly to her room, at the end of the hall. I looked at Nicole who had her head bent over the cups she was filling with water, watching the water, the bottom of the cup, the tea bag swelling in the cup and we could hear the sound of the water falling into the cups like water in fountains, and the steam too, the metallic sound when Nicole put the saucepan back on the stove, and her sigh, her eyes on the door and we heard Solange in her room, opening the chest of drawers, looking for something and rummaging through a whole pile of papers.

She didn't find what she was looking for. And she returned to us with a disappointed look, not angry but white and sad, so tired of having to keep talking when a simple letter would have told it all.

And she came back mumbling,

He's the only one of all my brothers, of all my brothers and sisters he's the only one,

And adding,

How many times did he write how sorry he was to have believed the priests' baloney about marriage and all that stuff when he was young. He didn't know what life was like. He knew nothing about life, he didn't understand, he wrote me that, and more than once. About Reine, yes. He could've kicked himself for wanting her to die and saying nasty things. And what about all the others who didn't say a thing, but thought that way, too. Believe me, Rabut, those people sleep better than you and me because for them a kid of seventeen who dies like that, it's her own damned fault; and that's the way it was back then, that's all, that's what they'll still say, and I—why are we talking about that, why am I talking to you about that? I don't want to talk about it—about old times. What's the use, talking about old times like that?

Rabut. What's the use of talking about that? Bernard is the way he is, he's the only one who never let me down.

I don't know, Solange. I don't know why we're talking about that.

I lowered my eyes as I spoke, just to find a breathing space and not force her to defend her brother again, and then Nicole took over, saying,

Yes, but meanwhile, what he did, what might happen to him.

And Solange not answering, not yet, not saying a word, nodding gently, smiling almost. And then she smiled openly, her face luminous at last.

Yes, a family of nuts, always has been, don't you think? Don't you think so, Rabut?

And that silence again, those words again, that wait again.

Anger, and once again not understanding. Telling yourself you're here waiting in a kitchen, telling yourself it's cold outside, it's night, and far from here, far from those days too, very far away there are reasons, connections, networks, invisible things working on us and we don't understand a thing about them.

Like telling yourself Woodsmoke's already waiting for us, I imagine, with his rifle and his bottle of wine next to him on the table. Yes, as soon as he got back to his place, he'll probably have started drinking again and waiting for us, knowing very well that someone will end up coming to him. Maybe he's waiting and drinking. Or just sitting there doing nothing, looking at the fire in his fireplace or talking to himself, to his dogs, still ruminating ideas of vengeance. Or, just as likely, thinking of his children and his wife, his years spent near Paris, and he's telling himself that his children over there in the Paris area only think of him as a dead man and this idea protects them from having to worry about him. Or even that they forgot his face. That they can hardly remember his voice and outbursts of anger against Mireille. We don't know who his children are or what they're doing, if they'll come here to ask about their family one day, or ask him for an explanation.

Because we're their family, we are, even if they don't know it, or don't want to know it, or were taught to reject us.

Because I don't think Mireille even dared slip in a word about us.

In the car afterward, when we got back, the only time we spoke, Nicole and I, was when I got mad at Solange because of this thought I had, this idea: hey, she went to get letters, letters he'd written her, for years.

For years, he wrote to Solange.

And when he came back, I mean, when he came back fifteen years after everybody else, it was as if for him the war had just ended. Because I also remember how we all came back, one after the other. And also how, very quickly, all of us, we went back to work so as not to think of it anymore, only take up life again with a kind of frenzy, we were so glad to be rid of those lousy places, the heat, the thirst, the dust, the laundry improvised at the bottom of a helmet, an old toothbrush to get the dirt off shirt collars, and the holes in your socks and your toes all bloody, that rotten world, and finally we were moving on, we wanted to make up for lost time, we'd wasted so much time over there, and also, what helped us, what helped me, I know, now I know, was when I learned one day that he wouldn't come home.

A simple telegram to his parents saying: I'm not coming back.

And it's true, that had helped me to concentrate all my attention on him and on what each of us could say about him, because we knew he'd met the daughter of a very rich colonist over there and he wanted to marry her. And we imagined him in the fancy neighborhoods of Paris, rich now, erasing the very memory of our names. Except that nobody even realized that Mireille's father no longer spoke to his daughter, or that the end of the colonies meant the end of the dowry, too.

But I really hung onto that and to the few gifts I'd given my parents, my sisters—gypsum flowers, a *caoua* set to serve coffee, and also a crucifix from Agadez for Nicole. That's right, our arms were filled with presents, with exoticism, with the magic of faraway places, postcards and our eyes filled with stars when we said to ourselves let's hope we don't hear the old guys grumbling yeah okay, but still,

It wasn't Verdun, your business over there.

And also the questions, dumber and dumber, questions nobody wanted to answer, about the weather, about farming, and women,

What are they like, under their veils?

The gross, idiotic jokes that revolted me,

Is it true that Muslim women shave their pussy?

Things like that.

And the desert, did you see the desert? The camels, how big is a camel?

Etc.

So to talk about him, about Woodsmoke, Bernard, was at least a good way not to have to talk at all.

We learned the rest from Solange: the wedding near Paris and how he settled in over there.

And then, it took a few years—I don't remember exactly how many, less than ten anyway, maybe seven or eight—when I heard from Février. Février, who'd decided to do the rounds. He'd wanted to say hello to the guys, the ones he remembered and stayed in touch with, in other words very few people. And when he came to visit for a couple of days at our house, he told me how he'd seen Bernard and Mireille at their place.

Yes, Février's the one who told me, when he came here to visit, with that need he had to go see his old buddies to find closure, he'd said, to put an end to something that was still bothering him.

My God, the things Février told me, things I would never have imagined.

But in the car, my anger at Solange: she always was so evasive, nodding her head vaguely to say that all those years she knew he was working at the Renault factory and had two children, living in a housing project, and that neither he nor his wife spoke to their family anymore and they had no friends, it was tough sometimes, but things were okay.

Except that it couldn't really have been that okay, of course, and he had said nothing about that to Solange. Since she, too, had been surprised, when she saw him turn up one day with no explanation.

And we all tried to understand, all of us.

I'd thought again of Février saying crazy things about Mireille, how in a housing project Mireille was no longer the arrogant girl, sure of herself, that we'd known in Oran, sucking up orangeades and the songs of Sacha Distel or Dario Moreno, her favorite singers, as she waited on a bar stool, painting her nails or nibbling on the tips of her big green sunglasses.

No, it's a whole different situation now, Février explained, when he came to see me and late in the evening, when we were alone and both slightly smashed since we'd been downing glass after glass of red wine, enough to betray the little promises we'd made to ourselves never to say what it was like over there, he ended up talking about Bernard and Mireille, telling me everything I didn't know, how he'd found them there, our two lovebirds from Oran, not so good-looking, not so young anymore, already tired and sad, making eyes at each other (more like murderous looks) and the worst possible words to blame each other for everything, Février had said, you should have seen them, especially her, resentful, bitter, pregnant with the second child.

Already she was a different woman from the sexy young pain in the butt all of us envied Bernard for: you envied your cousin too, didn't you, Rabut.

Watch how you're driving, you're hitting the curb. You're going too fast, watch out.

Yeah okay okay.

I slowed down a little. Nicole had spoken loudly, her voice suddenly frightened because she'd felt the car swerving to the right and going too fast. She'd put her hand on the wheel to straighten it out.

I'm telling you it's okay.

And then, ahead of us, there was the thin beam of the head-lights and nobody, not one car in the night. Only on the side of the road, fewer and fewer houses, set further and further apart. And then a few traffic circles and above all the snow falling furiously in thin little flakes, like dust particles or a swarm of gnats in summer under a streetlamp, in all directions, because of the wind. And then the sound of the engine and the two of us breathing in the car. Silence because we'd finally given up talking, Nicole looking to her right, maybe at her reflection, the night, the snow, her arms crossed while I was looking straight ahead and imagining what would happen early the next morning, when we'd have to meet Solange and the police on the church square to go to Bernard's place: what we'd say, what we'd do, all of us, together, in the cold, before heading for his house.

I could see already how we'd be early, Solange and me.

And maybe she'll even have called me ahead of time, to ask if the gendarmes were really needed. If the two of us. Or even if. If she herself, just her. If she, alone, couldn't get from him — what, exactly, she won't know. And then, there'll be silences on the phone. Through her voice, jolting in her throat, I'll hear her doubts, hesitations, and also her tiredness from her short night, against which she, too, must have been fighting, leaving her completely bewildered in the morning, trying to buck herself up by drinking cup after cup of coffee. She'll want to think that sleeping on it had led everyone to the same conclusion: do nothing, the gendarmes will give it all up, Chefraoui will forget the whole thing and even Bernard will apologize all by himself.

That's what she'll want to think, what she'll try to think, what she'll pretend to think possible.

And as I drove I could see Solange again walking us to the door and how she had stayed outside on the landing when we were telling her to go back in because of the cold. She had stood there watching us walk back to the car in front of the house.

We'd seen her with her body haloed in the yellow light from the electric bulb on the porch, her shawl over her shoulders and her arms crossed tight over her chest, looking at us but probably not even seeing us, already far off in her thoughts, her fears, her wait, and us leaving her alone with that huge night before her, until she resigned herself to go back in, turn off the outside light, and lock her door.

In the car I was saying to myself, what will Solange do now, will she go back to the little deep blue box on the kitchen table and push it off the table, brush it away with the back of her hand or only with her eyes, or even not touch it at all? Or, on the contrary, as with the shells left over from old wars that have to be defused, will she pick it up very cautiously and bring it back to the dining room or just ignore it and go into the bathroom to put on a nightgown and a bathrobe, listen to her fatigue and give herself up to it, or, why not, return to the living room, turn on the TV without even asking herself what programs they might have on a Saturday night and look at the images on the screen without understanding or seeing them.

Because she'll have to go to bed and not let herself be completely invaded by a few ideas, how many ideas a minute, how many new thoughts?

Maybe none.

But rage stiffening her body at the moment it's finally giving in to sleep, when behind the images of the day other images, other phrases will come through, words she'll try to imagine: her brother, the basement stairs, Chefraoui's wife struggling against him, shouting, defending herself.

And then she'll close her eyes so as not to see anymore, and she'll see even more. She'll pull up the sheet and blankets not to hear the voices of The Owl and Jean-Jacques anymore, and the exact opposite will happen, she'll hear them still more clearly, until it hurts, and she'll finally give up and turn on the bed lamp she had thought for a moment she could put out, as if she hadn't believed insomnia would take over soon.

Then she'll sit up in bed for a moment. Waiting for sleep to come.

And it won't come.

Because she'll sigh and hear herself claim Bernard wasn't always violent. She'll hear herself lie, trying to justify herself, and other voices whispering that she's cheating.

Then she'll stare straight ahead of her in her bed, she'll wait, and then finally it will be so late she'll think her trials will soon be over and sleep will come. She'll turn out the light, she'll stretch out, fluff up the pillow, and maybe before that go get a glass of water. Then she'll feel something like a jump in her chest again, she'll suddenly bristle at the injustice she thought had been done to Bernard all his life, bad luck, what bad luck, Solange, that's what I'll still be thinking as the car stops in front of our house.

So, Solange won't sleep well and I won't either, for sure.

She'll hear his voice, Bernard's voice. She'll hear it like I hear it now, like he could be heard and seen back in 1960, arriving at the draft center in Marseilles in his civilian clothes very early in the morning, after a night spent ruminating on his rancor. It's easy to picture him surprised that the train is so slow, that they don't have priority for going where they're going. That will vaguely irritate him, he doesn't like slowness.

Night will come, it comes, even if he doesn't care much about the night or the train or the draft notice he crumpled up and must be moldering at the bottom of one of his pockets—another drag, what's happening to him is just another drag, that's what he will have told himself so he won't have to think about it any more than necessary, since he wants to be completely focused on his anger and his ruminations.

And that's why he tries to isolate himself, so he can repeat the same words over and over, go around in circles over the money she's going to spend, his mother, she stole the money with no qualms whatsoever, he'll think, she'll spend my money without asking me, without saying a thing, with the money I won, me—the bundle of money he thought would let him leave his family and find a job as a mechanic or whatever, as long as it was somewhere else.

On the train, he sits quietly, or so it seems, without any particular expression, a few clothes in his wooden suitcase, a missal, nothing much really, just things he values, with his pants neatly pressed and his shoes too tight and still almost new. He has untied the laces, loosened the tongue, took his heel out of the shoe but didn't dare take his foot out completely. His face is carefully shaved and he has the smooth white skin of winter days, or of men who hardly ever shave. He's chewing on one of the sticks of gum he bought before he left. He has a pack in his pocket, with the cigarettes.

But what he's chewing and re-chewing, mostly, is his anger at his mother and the feeling he was cheated when he was there with his money, his check, no bank account and her to collect it.

That's right. He's a minor. He's still a minor.

He should have foreseen what was going to happen and arranged something with somebody else. He'd let her beat him to it, he was unprepared, off his guard; he keeps playing the picture of his mother in his mind, asking him to make out the check to her, in her name, since she has the family bank account. Bernard doesn't have an account yet, he'll have one when he's no longer a minor and works for real and not the way he does, helping on the farm or lending a hand to the neighbors. But she's the one who holds the money. She's the one they pay when he does a job for the neighbors; he doesn't pay rent at her house; he doesn't pay for his food in her house; he doesn't do his laundry either; it's only natural for them to pay her for his work. When he turns twenty-one, it'll be different.

In the meantime, the check will be in her name.

She gave him some money in an envelope, that'll help you out, she said to him. And she'll send him a little money every month, because it's well known that a soldier doesn't make much.

And he thinks of that again. The bitch, she's gonna spend it all, she'll start by buying two animals because for months she resented not being able to buy them, a dead loss, the expenses for milk, and then she'll be able to replace the two others and I'll still have to say thank you for the crumbs she'll send me every month, he tells himself.

That's it, he didn't say a thing. He berates himself for not having said anything and acting like a kid, letting himself be swindled by the envelope and thrown off balance by an unexpected gesture on her part, when he got some money to round off his pay. That's what being a minor means, you depend on your parents, you're not eligible to vote but you are eligible for the *djebels*.

The *djebels*. For all he knows about them. Just a word he heard one Sunday at the market.

And now he's leaving on a train that's too slow, where young men like himself are piled up, sniggering or silent. He looks at them distrustfully. He has no intention of talking to anyone, and certainly not of answering that young guy who's asking him if he has any information about what's going on over there, if he knows whether it's true or not—you get your throat cut just like that, or is it stuff they say to scare the rookies?

He says he doesn't have a clue, but he doesn't add that, above all, he doesn't give a damn.

He doesn't feel concerned. Maybe he makes a face that doesn't mean anything. His mind is elsewhere—what she'll do with his pile of cash, he's sure of it, she's going to spend it, the bitch, and this time he could really see that she understood how much she could hurt him.

And all night long, in the jolts of the train, all he does is brood over the vengeance that will come sooner or later, and he'll recover his money, he promises that to himself, promises himself to think about it every single day, I'll never cave in, he tells himself. And he thinks the months ahead of him won't break his determination: he'll put in his months and he'll come back, that's all.

And when the train stops in the morning, it's not Marseilles, it's a little station. The bustle, so much agitation, he has a hard time understanding. As if he were a stranger in a country where the language was as foreign to him as the customs. He's not asleep, but he's not awake either. He hears the doors opening noisily, then there's the metallic glare of the iron, and then the footsteps, the voices of the men who're laughing and acquainted already, they'll say they're friends before quickly forgetting each other, somewhere in a country of which they know nothing.

And he follows the crowd, but slowly, groping in his pocket to see if he still has his pack of cigarettes and his gum. He checks his suitcase, you never know, and he must have slept, in fact he feels spongy, cottony, he sees the world like you do when you have a fever and everything resembles the numbness of the first hours of sleep, or after a dream, almost.

The car was full of guys like him, the bewildered look of the youngest, or the skinniest, with their pale faces only colored on their cheeks by acne. They all thought they'd see Marseilles, the sun, and soon the sea. An image from a picture postcard, a port drenched in sunlight and the dazzling reflections in the water, like aluminum foil.

But they have arrived in a station that isn't Marseilles, a station that's too small. And it's still too dark out, they can't see much in the early morning except the massive dark silhouettes of the trucks into which they're going to be loaded, very quickly, as if on the sly—and the canvas-covered trucks will drive on with nobody really talking, overwhelmed, all of them.

And at that moment even he will stop thinking about his mother, or of what he could have done with his money if he hadn't gotten that draft notice.

It's very early in the morning and he's hungry. But instead of a cup of coffee and a meal, like everybody else he gets a metal tag. He understands, he's already been told what that is,

A soldier, that's it, you're a soldier, almost, not quite: you still have a name but soon you'll only be the number on the tag around your neck, on the metal that will burn your skin sometimes, during the scorching afternoons, or on the contrary, will be too cold; the tag you'll never forget, your first gift from the army. On the metal two numbers separated by dotted holes. And if you die, soldier, a piece of it will be cut out by one of your buddies who was luckier than you were, and a gendarme will take it to your family with all that remains of you.

So it gives him a funny feeling when he looks at it, and he tells himself that he's already played the lottery, he doesn't like the idea of doing it again, even if he doesn't understand what will happen soon, because over his head the sky is blue and the air is sweet. He tells himself that back home the sky must be gray as dust, like it always is, like so often, like the water into which he has to throw his tray. Back there the sky is gray and the food's worse than here. But he doesn't trust the barracks they make you stay in, that camp universe, barracks lined up one after the other, gloomy, everything's gloomy under the blue sky, he never would've believed it: it's not enough to have a blue sky, the huge cafeteria where he finally had a decent meal but alone, isolating himself from the others, from the little groups that have started to form, where some guys are already boasting, talking, and making trouble.

And he can hear what they're saying and what the old men in the villages keep saying and what they repeat here to buck themselves up,

Yeah, well, it's not Verdun,

Twenty-eight months is a long time but it's not Verdun, that's for sure, and they say they have whorehouses here.

They laugh, they snicker, they drive their fear away by pretending it's all right.

As for him, he just eats and thinks, twenty-eight months, hang on for twenty-eight months and every day, every hour, every minute he'll have to be focused on demanding every single centime of his money, coin after coin, and she'll do anything she can to say she doesn't owe him anything, of course that's what she'll want to do, take advantage of the situation, take advantage of him, and the purpose of every day should be to remind him of his obligation not to cave in, not to let go, too easy for her, for all of them back there, to take advantage of him while he's over here doing God knows what with God knows who, God knows where.

But God has nothing to do with it.

God can help him, a little, when he'll find the time to open his suitcase and pick up his missal with the edge colored not cabbage green but patched up with old brown insulating tape, and slip it into his pocket, hold it tight against him and sometimes read a little, two or three words, psalms whose every passage he knows by heart, but he'd rather read them to keep his eyes away from what surrounds him, the din of the loudspeakers spitting out announcements, the sniggers, the complaints, the shouting matches and those ghastly bunk beds swarming with bedbugs, fleas, crabs too, and from time to time some of them give a yell because they can hear rats squeaking, and it all stinks of urine and mold.

Hygiene leaves a lot to be desired and the evening seems to last all night. Sleep does not come, you stay huddled over your suitcase, the precious suitcase with your snapshots and your knick-knacks, your souvenirs like relics ripped from the world you come from, supposed to embody a daily life that has already retreated into the distance in just a few hours, because of all the strange things you've seen, like those men who've returned from over there for a few days with their bags full of oddities, gifts, people say they have money, too, and they're cautious, even prickly, as soon as you get too close to their food. But he has no intention of approaching them; he, too, wants to be left alone. Besides, he, too, worries about his suitcase, he's reluctant to leave it alone under the blanket of his scruffy bed.

And when they ask him for his movement order—it's an officer who's ordering him to present it—he hesitates, says to himself he doesn't know what the man's rank is, or how you recognize them or what his own rank is for that matter—necessarily the lowest—he thinks the man has a Marseilles accent because we're near Marseilles. And when the man demands to see his movement order again, he goes livid. He doesn't know where it is anymore. So he has to run back and find his suitcase. Back to his barracks and the strong, nauseating stench of sweat hits him as he goes in. And also the silence, suddenly the silence he would love to have at night, but will dissipate as the men fill up the room. And as he goes to his bed he worries about finding his suitcase, his things, what if they'd been stolen, what would become of him, what would he be punished for, without papers, without anything to prove his identity, unable to satisfy the officer who's waiting out there. And when he comes running back to the officer he hardly looks at the paper Bernard holds out to him. He's given the order to join the two guys who are repainting white lines on the curbs of the sidewalks. They have to be white. Always white, until others come to relieve him.

So he obeys without thinking. He even finds some comfort in doing that. The idiocy of the job, the doggedness you need for it and he finds inside himself to focus on the task, no matter how absurd it is, even if it has to be repeated every hour because every hour the boots leave prints, like skid marks on the freshly painted curbs, not quite dry.

And it must be done again, no big deal, retouch with white, and with the two other guys who're also on the detail, they walk around all day long with a paint bucket in their hands and their eyes fixed on the curbs of the sidewalks, all around the camp, and the camp is very big, the curbs keep coming, they make arabesques he looks at until he drowns in them, until he can't see the bustle of the camp around him anymore.

It's only when one of the two draftees talks about the officer who assigned them to this detail that Bernard raises his head

99

again. He feels embarrassed and silly, and maybe he even blushes at his ignorance when he hears the other guy making fun of the officer's accent, because the Alsatian accent really is horrible. And he smiles with the two others, says nothing about the accent, so that accent was Alsatian, a long way from Marseilles. At least he knows that, he remembers how far Alsace is from Marseilles, he learned it in school, a long time ago.

In another life.

He holds his paintbrush, leans down, and all day long he keeps repainting over the footprints and the streaks left by shoe rubber. He raises his eyes from time to time, he tells himself it's better to be busy with his brush and paint than to try to avoid work details and officers. It'll take as long as it takes, that's all. That's something at least, filling the time to get through the day, then through another one, waiting for the evening and another, yet another, before they leave, on the fourth evening.

As if they had to sneak out of France with their suitcases in their hands again and now the additional rolled-up khaki blanket on their shoulder, and find themselves on the docks at night, on a clear but cold evening, ready to get on board.

And now he's there, on the docks of La Joliette in Marseilles. They chalked the number of his regiment on his helmet. He's tired, he hasn't slept. He hopes he'll get some sleep and yet he still has to bear the fatigue and the agitation around him, in his unit, all the units that are going to board tonight, with only a few idlers who have come to see them off from afar, hardly calling out a few good-byes, like bread crumbs to the fish and birds of the port.

And this time, telling himself he's going to see the sea, even if it's at night. Just too bad it has to be at night. He's going to see the sea and he's thinking of the first words he'll write Solange. He tells himself he'll talk about the size of the ship, a ship so big, he'll say, that you could almost fit all the people of La Bassée into it. But he won't talk about the eyes of the men around him, the strange silence that has filled their eyes and, on the boat with them, with the cold air lashing at them, the presence of fear.

But he'll be able to talk about the seagulls busying themselves around the tugboats like flies around the horses and cows in summer; and he won't talk about the tension, the panic suddenly in everyone's eyes, their bodies contracting, their gestures slowing down, their breath held back, when, louder than the voices and shouts of the few men on the docks, even louder than the cries of the gulls—those few gulls gliding over their heads like the little warplanes he saw once in the newsreels—still louder, yes, all the way into your throat, into your head, impossible to say that and even more to write it, he'll think, not to Solange and not to anyone, when under his feet there is something like a tremor, a movement, voices, and the wind, and the gulls, and he senses a longer, louder sound resonating in the very depths of his being, it seems to him, it even makes his hands sweat and for once he meets the livid gaze of another draftee who, like him, like them, knows that from that moment on, his whole life will be perforated by the sound of the siren announcing their departure.

NIGHT

WHAT HAPPENS—FIRST, HOW VERY FAST THE SOLDIERS smash in the doors and charge into the houses with their guns in their hands, the houses so low, so dark it takes time for the eyes to get used to it and find only a few women and old men, sometimes children deep inside the rooms.

Not one able-bodied man.

The soldiers sweep through the village yelling as they run, they yell to buck themselves up, to frighten, like rattling groans, hard breathing, so the old women let go of the baskets they're weaving and look at the young men, surprised that with guns in their hands they're the ones who seem frightened. They're angry, they yell,

Out!

Out!

And in the houses they grab people by the arms, pull on their clothing,

Get out! Get the fuck out!

And the women put down the baskets. They get up. They leave the looms, they walk out, the old men walk out, they don't know why and their slow steps contradict their obedience, with their raised hands flat on their heads and the barrels of the automatic rifles pushing them towards the center of the village.

The children walk forward too, looking up at the soldiers, their faces are contorted, they're holding back, fear keeps them from crying.

Children are screaming in front of the door of a house. They remain motionless, two little ones, just standing there, they scream until a woman comes to get them and brings them with her to sit in the town square, squeezed together, all of them, neighbors, friends, all the others, family, all of them, as long as they're women, old people, children, all huddled together at the level of the soldiers' legs, with the tips of the barrels dancing before their eyes and the stifling hot dust, thick, white, blurring eyes and smells, and leaving a dry floury taste in the mouth.

Hens cluck across the village square and scrabble around in the dust and dogs are barking, you can hear goats, and the doors being smashed in, women's screams, a few women locked in or hidden, young women dressed in bright colors, red, blue, yellow, they resist, they have to be pushed, pushed at gun point and you have to yell,

Fuck, move it!

Then bring them back to the square,

Come on!

More violently than the old people because they know something, they know where the men are.

The men, where the hell are the men?

No one can find the men.

The old people don't talk either, remain silent—only the toothless mouths vibrate and make a lapping sound and splutter, or quiver like the fingers hooked onto the canes that are holding them up. Aside from that the eyes say nothing, nothing, not even astonishment. Not even anger, nothing. Calm, resignation, nothing, patience, perhaps. Some of them saw the bodies after the napalm bombings — the little black heaps of charred bodies with their limbs intact, others had their penis split by electric shocks, they miraculously escaped death, they saw soldiers stone men to death and twelve-year-old girls give themselves to the soldiers without crying; so now they're not afraid and they wait, patience is on their side.

The lieutenant is talking with Abdelmalik, one of the two *harkis*. Now he's bawling at the top of his lungs at those bitches who don't want to talk, we'll make them talk, they'll have to talk, them or the old guys,

Fuck it, they have to talk.

And while he's yelling and spitting and wiping his forehead with the back of his sleeve, they keep searching the houses and forcing open the possible weapons caches, the doors, more doors, a few more, of the houses slightly set back from the street, and from the inside you can hear breaking, things being knocked down, hens run away, goats scatter, maybe there'll be weapons in the big earthen jars they smash open and only find wheat that spreads over the floor like powder or sand in clouds of yellow dust between the fingers.

Février wants to go into one of the last houses and the door won't open. It's resisting. Three or four together, it's got to give way. And inside there is a woman and a blind old man who jumps when the door gives way and floods the room with light and the soldiers figure right away the old man's blind because he's the only one who doesn't turn his face to them.

But he's not the one you walk up to. Nor to the woman, who might be the blind man's daughter, but to the two children, almost not children anymore, a girl and a boy, fourteen or fifteen, not the age of a *fellagha* yet.

How we know he's not a fell, how we know what he is, guys?

What are you?

Say it, say what you are.

We asked you a question.

You don't speak French? No, you don't understand?

The adolescent doesn't say anything, he shrinks back slightly, hardly one step, and he looks at the soldiers one after the other. He makes a sign to say he doesn't understand, he raises his arms and wants to put them on his head, then changes his mind, lowers them down to his body, then, in Arabic, he says words nobody understands. You can feel, you can guess what he means. He must be saying he doesn't understand and doesn't know what they're asking, while his eyes are just saying he's terrified—and he's going to try to alleviate his fear by looking at his mother and sister, by looking at the old man. Nobody seems to understand what he's saying.

Where you hiding weapons?

Where're you hiding weapons, say it.

The first time they hit him he doesn't flinch, he barely even starts, or blinks. His voice is shaking, that's all, to say he doesn't understand or he's not hiding anything, or whatever, other words, impossible to make out.

The weapons?

Where are they, say it.

He looks at them and doesn't answer.

The men, where're they hiding?

No, he makes a sign to say no.

Where, you know where.

Say it.

He shakes his head to say no.

The fells, you don't know anything?

There are two soldiers very close to him and they give him little slaps with their fingertips, on his skull, behind his head, on the nape of the neck.

The weapons, where are they?

He closes his eyes, his eyes blink. The sharp sound of slaps. The boy still stands straight. He holds his breath. The sounds of slaps get louder and louder, on the cheeks, on the eyes, on his forehead, he knits his brows, you can see his jaw muscles shuddering, he holds his breath, he makes a gesture of not knowing and he says no with a sharp, nervous movement, like a spasm. He steps back. He spreads out his hands and puts his arms up. They search him and find nothing under his clothing but the trembling of his whole body and the cold sweat on the back of his rigid neck, and as soon as the hitting stops he opens his eyes wide and his breath makes his chest rise and he breathes very loudly through his nose, with his mouth open.

Outside, the sound—they listen—of more doors being kicked in. You can hear the big clay jars thrown down, smashing apart on the ground. And children, babies crying. And dogs barking. Then a shot. They jump. Goats. A dog, someone killed a dog. And they search the adolescent. Then the others. Then someone gropes the girl's djellaba. Then the girl looks at her mother as her hair escapes from the headscarf that the soldier slides off, and her hair comes undone, falls over her shoulders. Then she opens her mouth as if to express surprise. She clenches her fists. The soldier lingers, searching, groping her breasts for a long time. Mouret and Février watch without saying anything. Then Février walks up to the girl, the other soldier moves over, Février touches the djellaba and stops when the girl lets out a soft cry, almost nothing, and then takes refuge in silence. Her anger must be kept in the background—she knows, she repeats to herself that she can't lose her head, above all she can't get mad, she can't scream, she absolutely can't scream, can't insult them, you have to wait, have to keep quiet.

Mouret looks at Février and motions him to drop it.

Février turns away and goes back to the boy,

You don't want to say anything?

You don't want to talk? We'll make you talk, you know we can make you, you know that?

He walks over, he hesitates. He looks the boy in the eyes then spits right next to him. He looks at the boy again, as if he wanted to tell him something, or understand him, or probe into his silence, into his fear, and grab something, read a confession in it, secrets; and he looks at the old man and the woman, but now all he can see is wrinkled, furrowed skin and the man has eyes as dead as his youth.

Then Février gets almost scared and his eyes finally alight on the girl. She's holding up the top of her djellaba with one hand and with the other she's trying to hold back her hair. She does not focus on Février's eyes, nor on the others'. They make the boy put his two hands flat on his skull. He's crying, silently, the tears fog up his eyes, and flow down his cheeks. There is no revolt or anger in his expression. The blind man does not move at all and neither does the mother, she barely turns her face away, lowers her eyes a little. As for the boy, his wide-open eyes are on the men— eyes open and shining as if they were reflecting a hallucination.

And still from outside you can hear babies crying, another dog barking, women wailing, and then that burnt smell spreading out, and on the square, the cries of the women and the lamentations also floating in the acrid, bitter smell of the black smoke, the smell, the smoke filtering in and soon stinging nostrils and eyes.

The men are going to leave. They are going to go out. Février hesitates and looks at the girl, she can feel it, the others feel it too, the soldiers too. Mouret gives him a punch in the shoulder.

Come on, let's go.

They walk out. They're on the doorstep when Nivelle turns around with no warning, a sharp, mechanical movement without thinking it seems, he retraces his steps, a few strides, his body stiff; he walks a few meters and takes his gun out of his belt and without looking without thinking straight ahead walks up to the boy and puts a bullet in his head.

Outside, Février and the others discover the village in flames. The women and the old people are in the middle of the square, while from some burning houses comes the sound of moaning. And all the men and women are sitting next to each other, huddled one against the other, and the women are crying, not all of them, some of them turn around and look at the burning houses, and others are imploring; the men lower their eyes and wait, their hands flat on their heads, they wait and the crying of the women is even more unbearable than the smoke and the fire devastating the houses around them, more unbearable perhaps than the soldiers so close to them, aiming their machine guns at them, and the lieutenant shouting and circling around them, he kicks shoulders, backs, and he orders them to talk, to tell where the able-bodied men are, you know where, the husbands, sons, brothers, of course you know where, since they abandoned you here,

They're dogs, the lieutenant repeats, dogs because they abandoned you, they knew we'd come and they abandoned you.

And he keeps circling the group of men and women and children, and then soldiers walk between them, step over the bodies, and kick them at random, hard boot-kicks, the women are howling and the children are crying in their arms. They yell they don't know,

We don't know anything, the men left so long ago, we don't know, to the city, to Oran, for work, they left to look for work.

And the lieutenant does not believe them. The soldiers do not believe them. The lieutenant tears a baby from a woman's arms — at first she resists, she holds the child back, her arms, her hands clinging to the body of the child and a soldier comes to help the lieutenant, pushing away the woman, hitting her on the arms and shoulders with his rifle butt, so she'll let go, so she'll give in, and finally she gives in and collapses and the lieutenant takes the baby, he picks it up by the neck with one hand, brandishes it in the air, the old men and the women sit up but the soldiers point their barrels and the lieutenant raises his arm higher still and they can see the baby and the tiny arms, tiny legs kicking around,

His father, where is he, where's his father?

And the lieutenant keeps standing with his arm up and the child screams and struggles, he looks like he's swimming, his mother screams, she implores them, she has crawled up to the lieutenant's feet and wants to hang on to him but the soldier hits her again with his rifle butt, pushes her away, the lieutenant doesn't see her, he looks at the others in the square, all the others, sitting there, terrified, not daring to move,

Where are they, where are your men?

And he doesn't wait for an answer, it's over, he takes out his gun and slaps the mouth of the barrel onto the baby's temple and a pink mark shows on the temple, deep in it, and the baby screams, the lieutenant looks at the women, at the old men, they say nothing and he looks at the soldiers around him, frozen, very pale too,

No,

He hears a voice saying

No,

And he waits like that, and he lets the silence cover everything, then he wonders if it's him, if he's the one who has spoken and said,

No.

He puts his gun back in the holster, and with an indifferent gesture, like a pit you spit out after rolling it around in your mouth for a long time, he throws the baby a few meters away from him; and soon you hear only tears and the endless wailing of the woman who throws herself on the child.

And then they'll keep going, to the next village.

From one village to the next, still the smell of the smoke, not only on clothes but in the air, spreading out and coloring the sky. They go through the cool of an immensely wide stream for a while, but the water is only a very thin trickle winding along a bed of pebbles that have to be stepped over, like the loose stones and the tufts of thistles. The earth is moist, sandy, dotted with pickleweed. You can hear sheep and goats. There are traces of sandals and hiking boots. They walk fairly fast, in silence, with only the sound of water between the stones and the pebbles sliding underfoot, the voices, when they say shit, voices of men stumbling and the clink of metal junk in the loads the guys are carrying.

A stop to put your hands in the water, refresh yourself.

Nobody says anything. And when the lieutenant orders Poiret to go get the ones who're lagging behind, he grumbles a little, not out of fear, but out of scorn for the ones lagging behind, or simply because he doesn't want to walk more than he has to.

And of course Châtel's the one he finds alone, last. When he sees him coming toward him his look is unmistakable,

Leave me alone.

Châtel would like to say,

Leave me alone.

But he doesn't say it. Except through the whiteness, the pale-ness of his face, his cold look. Or, rather, angry look. Furious now. And then it doesn't last long. The time for the others to turn around when they hear not voices, not the sound of hands but the gear of the two men falling into the water and the splash-ing of the bodies fighting and the pebbles rolling around in the water.

When they're separated, Châtel is on the ground, the other is insulting him and keeps hitting, he hits hard, kicks. Châtel is in the water protecting his face, his body feels nothing, barely feels the pebbles under him rolling, sliding, striking his body, his back, buttocks and legs, not even Poiret's kicks,

Come on, fight, you fucking piece of shit, fight!

And then the others hold Poiret back, they help Châtel get up and gather his things.

But roughly, without any friendship for him, just to go faster, because the lieutenant had given the order. And they don't look at him. You wouldn't be surprised if he started to cry. But he doesn't cry. He walks along and mumbles something, his eyes fixed on the back of the ones walking in front of him, as if he couldn't see anything anymore and the shade they're enjoying for the moment would last forever.

But no. Soon you have to leave the wadi. You can see the roofs of the next village.

Châtel comes to a halt and starts throwing up.

That evening, he's standing at the bar of the rec hall, and for a time that seems to last forever, he stays there without moving, his elbows on the bar, his eyes turned to the room.

Nivelle and Poiret are playing foosball there.

Châtel looks at them and can't take his eyes off those two guys he doesn't understand.

He looks at them, the way they both have of holding their arms in front of them and keeping their legs wide apart, their torsos and shoulders very mobile, the back of Nivelle's neck, their skulls under the crew cut hair. He sees them turning the handles, he hears the clacking of the chromed bars and the clacks resound in the thick, heavy silence of this room which is suddenly too subdued, where the men are drinking their beer without talking— they don't talk, they smoke, and they have in their voices, when they need to talk, a sort of slowness. Is it fatigue, is it fear, he doesn't know. He can still hear and feel the water in the wadi and the stones rolling under his skin when the other guy was demanding that he fight, in that voice he hears yelling the same way at Nivelle now, exactly the same way, because he's winning; and the noise of the ball when it seems to cut through the opponent's goal, a quick sharp sound like the shot of a gun.

Châtel jumps.

Both of them are playing with such frenzy that sometimes the whole foosball table moves, and Châtel is almost frightened by that. And the looks of the other men around him, how they're watching the two of them playing like maniacs, their resounding voices, the scraping of the frame over the floor, the white balls rolling and thrown with a sure hand into the middle of the playing field.

And later when Châtel walks into the barracks, when all the others are still hanging out a little longer in the rec hall before heading for dinner, he sees Bernard sitting on his bed, absorbed in his missal.

And if Bernard raises his head, it's to plunge it back into his book and let his lips run from one psalm to another, holding his breath, completely concentrated. Châtel knows that he can talk to no one here, not even to Bernard, as he had first thought. It's over, he knows it, Bernard is irritated by Châtel, everything in him annoys him, his strange thinness and pallor, his thin black mustache over his lips, a sort of very fine down, like a shadow, which he trims with scissors every day. Too sure of himself behind that fragile look that serves as a screen, as false modesty, and that look of a student he has, of an intellectual, his ugliness, too, which makes Bernard think that it's probably because women don't like him that Châtel can easily see himself as a servant of God.

Because Châtel is something of a pacifist, one of those people Bernard knows only because of a few words he heard somewhere, the kind of people nobody has ever known personally; Châtel is someone who thinks that one God doesn't necessarily exclude another, that you can have other beliefs and yet the same rights, who sometimes even says,

The UN, you know what the UN is?

It's impossible to talk to him, he and Bernard agree about nothing.

All the same, that evening, when both of them are called, among others, Bernard can guess how lonely Châtel's going to feel, even more than the other men, and yet they'll have to go, step into the night with all the others, then leave the base, walk a good thirty meters and spread out around it—they don't like that, no one likes that, because you find yourself alone in the night and you have to stay awake and on the alert for hours, squatting or standing with your rifle in your hand.

They form a circle around the base, but the links of the chain are so spaced out that you know you're alone, the space between two men is now so wide, so vast, you can't talk to the others, at first you'd like to talk to someone but when you learn that talking makes you a target and smoking too, that you can be seen and heard, you give up very quickly and right away you feel more naked and vulnerable than inside the base, here nothing protects you—and for Bernard, as for the others, the only company is the horrible rumblings that tear his stomach apart, the urge to vomit and hunger too, because dinner is already well behind him, the food is so bad, well, no, not bad really, but it's always so much the same thing. Because you'd like, the body would like to know something besides the corned beef or the cans of tuna in oil or the dried vegetables and rice again, always rice, or the boiled beef soup in which for days on end they find the same lousy, spoiled meat that passes for beef,

Come on, this is beef?

rages Février, who knows something about beef and can tell the taste of lamb or camel right away. But he doesn't recognize the taste of the donkeys they occasionally kill by mistake here—corpses of animals whose only virtue is not to come from a can. So, meat. And wine. And going home. That's what Février talks about to Bernard, in the evening, when he shows the pictures of his fiancée in his wallet. Because here, women are souvenirs tucked into wallets where the Saturday night dances, the fiancées they've held tight, light dresses and springtime warmth are stored, and then comes the throbbing pain of desire, a desire they drive away by joking around.

But Février shows a picture of Éliane at the beach, you see her standing, she's smiling at the photographer and every time he shows it, he knows it may be to boast a little, to say yes, look at the girl who's waiting for me, her legs and her pretty naked feet in the sand, the bikini and her hair in the wind and her hands on her hips and that smile on the beach of Tranche-sur-Mer, her breasts thrust out and the whole barracks whistles,

Send us home, for chrissake!
And Février shouts,
Home, for chrissake!
And they all laugh,
Home, for chrissake!

They try to rip the snapshot away from him, to pass it around, and comments fly between two laughs.

And now, in the night, the cold finally gets to you.

Bernard tries to shift position often, his limbs go numb and he tries to hear the men to his right and to his left, the ones who are shifting position like him and you can hear from far off.

You tell yourself it's them, because even if your eyes get used to the night, what you're on the lookout for, at first, what he, too, tries to hear rather than see, is all the sounds that don't come from him, from his body whose breathing is so heavy that sometimes that's what scares him, as if someone were breathing behind him, as if there were someone right next to him—and so hands and fingers grip the rifle very hard, eyes strain to spot a shadow in the darkness, a shape—but what emerges in the bluish gray is the outline of the landscape you've known for months but at night you'd rather see it from up there, when you're a sentry, rather than out here at the outpost.

The difference is that up there you're in a stone tower, solid, firm, made of gray stones that have no fear of bullets, and you climb up there through a staircase you access through a steel door, locked by the commanding officer. There's nothing to be scared of up there; you tell yourself that if the base were attacked, it's probably the only place where nothing could happen to you.

Sometimes, when Bernard is on sentry duty with the night stretched out in front of him, the cold doesn't keep him awake.

It's mild out, you could even fall asleep more easily than in the barracks, because here, at least, neither the snores nor the smells of sweat disturb your craving for sleep. The cicadas help move you toward sleep, that gentle floating, too, that you feel, of the wind in the trees and the brush, that numbness whose caress you get to like very quickly, telling yourself: this could be a lot worse.

You imagine what's happening on the other side of the base, behind the big oil tanks. You imagine the sea and the ships whose sirens can sometimes be heard in the distance, and on the other side, behind the hills, you tell yourself that this country stretches out, a country you only know by name and the ideas people have about it, postcard clichés, the desert, the camels, one imagines turbaned horsemen galloping down the trails at top speed, the sand kicking up like a cloud around them and broad, supple movements when they twirl their huge, curved, sickle-shaped sabers high above their heads.

But for now you cling to your rifle and Bernard, like the others, is ruining his eyes looking for shapes moving in the night.

Wild dogs do come prowling around, he knows that very well, he can spot them sometimes from his sentry post in the tower— brown spots sticking out in the transparent blue, pinkish in some places—but from up there you're not afraid of being attacked, not even by the dogs attracted by the smell of the garbage cans.

Whereas now, this very evening, you'll hear a slight cracking sound first.

Like twigs cracking under footsteps.

For a few seconds Bernard holds his breath, he wants to hear. He wonders if it's not just a buddy taking a leak further on— often, when he's here, he's so scared of being attacked precisely at the moment when he lets his guard down to take a piss that he holds it back as long as he can—you have so many stories in your head—so many guys like him found in the early morning with their throat slashed open and their member in their mouth. So he strains his ears even more, yes, a noise still pretty far away, like twigs being crushed, or is it the wind—he's well aware it might be just about anything.

There are so many nights he can't manage to sleep, even inside the base.

It's because he's still outraged by that business with the money and his mother: he knows he can't do anything about it.

And it's no use trying to drive fear away in the night by reciting psalms and stroking the metal or tapping the butt of his automatic rifle, he knows that for weeks, the first weeks at least, anger blinded him and how, thanks to it, or because of it, like an anesthetic, he hadn't even realized until now that he had boarded that ship. Because for him there's no way he's going to go back to the fields, or sit for whole afternoons watching cows graze away his youth and his whole life slipping away from him in the rustling of the poplar leaves.

All that's over and done with.

Now he dreams of having a trade, being a mechanic, working in a city and leaving the boredom and fatigue of the fields behind. He wants money. He imagines that with money everything will change. He'll be able to leave for the city and find a job in a factory or even, why not, in a garage, like Nivelle, who's a mechanic in a car dealership near Orléans. Or better still, ever since he met Mireille: have his own garage. That's what he dreams about and sometimes talks about with other people, because some of them understand the idea of not going back to the farm, since the work is hard and doesn't necessarily pay off.

And he thinks again of the money no sooner won than lost.

He can see himself demanding the money from his mother the day after he gets back, after he finally got some sleep and had some food to find the strength to oppose her and calmly claim his due. It can't happen the day they pick him up at the station, when everybody will want to touch him, as if to make sure it's really him standing there in front of them. He can see it all, he can even imagine the face of his mother who'll be waiting for him at home, he won't speak to her right away, but the day after he gets back, trembling, stiff, ready to give up because of the fear in his belly and yet determined not to give in and to demand that she give him back, coin after coin, the exact amount of which nothing will be left but two cows in a field and the brand new roof on the barn.

He thinks of all that, especially during the night.

And now he tells himself he won't recover the money his mother took from him. He doesn't need it anymore. He tells himself he's damned if he'll ever set foot in La Bassée again, still less in his parents' house, because now he knows Mireille and he knows he'll leave with her and open up his garage in Paris.

And this time, he's almost sure of it, there's something out there, far off, something moving.

Something coming toward him.

He squats down and waits. He wants to hear better, behind the sounds of the cicadas and the blowing of the wind, soft as it is and so warm, under a sky too clear for the fells to risk—what, we'd see them, we'd probably see them, the sky too pale, cloudless, the moon half full and the stars like millions of flashlights—yes, he looks ahead of him, he can see a little and even sees himself very well, his hands, arms, legs, body, the gray light reflected on the metal of his gun. It's not a very dark night, so he tells himself they won't dare. And besides, the only time they dared, he remembers, he was in the barracks and suddenly the night was cut sharply in two by a burst of machine gun fire, like a fruit sliced by the blade of a knife.

The eyes of all the men had opened wide as if they were the eyes of one single man.

Everybody waking up at once with a start, and silence, the time to sit up in bed, turn on the light and listen, shut up the men who were talking and worrying without even giving themselves time to understand.

Shut the fuck up!

They were watching each other, trying to hold their breath, already breathing heavily, loudly, almost panting.

Shut up!

And then the bursts of gunfire had resumed in the night. They had said: it's the guy up there in the sentry box, it's him firing, he's just answering their fire.

For a few seconds they'd wondered if it was an attack, if they'd have to fight, or if.

Then nothing. Silence. Very long, very deep. As if the whole coast had silenced all life to let the bullets pierce the thickness of the dark and the coolness of the air; and then a jackal—unless it wasn't a jackal but the rallying cry of the fells, they thought of that. And then nothing.

The next day, they'd found bootprints in the ground and a huge puddle of blood, black as oil, and then the lifeless body of a local guy in blue overalls they knew very well.

So he thinks of that night again and now he knows it's a bad idea, he shouldn't think about it, they won't come. It's too light out. The night is too bright. He does hear someone coughing further off, though, as if someone were talking behind him.

He turns around and behind him there is only the mass of the lookout tower and the gate of the base, and he pivots halfway round again, he knows you shouldn't stay like that, with your back to the hills. He feels fear gaining on him, because he isn't cold at all anymore, and it even seems a sticky sweat is spreading over his back, invading him almost completely.

He passes his hand over his neck and forehead, yes that's it, a sticky liquid, no need to taste it, he knows its salty taste by heart.

There must be something you can do, like think about Mireille, that's what you need, to hold out, not yield to fear and the urge to piss, he'll have to give in to it pretty soon, but not yet. For the moment he can hold out and he's going to stand there, cling to his rifle, pivot around a few times and not count the shadows or the shapes, the outlines, the angles, the trees, the movements of the branches or the number of hills or anything else, but think about Mireille and tell himself again he loves her and also that love is no big deal.

He doesn't think about Mireille all the time. He doesn't think she's a very beautiful girl. No, love is not blind, not like they say.

He pictures himself in a garage, he'd be the boss and Mireille would keep the books, she'd know how to do that, for sure; he thinks back to their meeting in a bar with his cousin Rabut, how he'd forgotten his army cap and for that reason she'd written him, and also invited him to come over to her house and pick it up. And how impressed he had been by Mireille's father when he and Février found themselves sitting on the chairs they had been offered, over a glass of orangeade (as if they were children and not men).

They couldn't help thinking that not only had they never seen a peasant and winegrower like Mireille's father, but they would even have doubted his existence, doubted the very possibility of his existence—a farmer with such delicate white hands—if they hadn't been there, in front of him, sitting around a big table of shiny black wood, with him in a shirt and tie, his sleeves rolled high up on his forearms, with a rather relaxed look and yet a severe, almost austere face, with his hair combed back, his glasses emphasizing his bony but ordinary face, without anything that really distinguished him from the other French colonists here.

But all those paintings on the walls, the Arab woman who came to open the door. And the rugs. The patio with its fountain. The coolness. And the large pieces of furniture. The staircase. The whole house, so vast, he tells himself that all this is part of Mireille's beauty. And then he hears Mireille tell him that she thinks he kind of looks, no, in fact he does look like an American actor whose name he can't even remember. And he tells himself all this. Repeats it to himself. Tells himself that maybe Mireille is his chance to make it.

Yes, she really is his chance. He's sure of it.

And when he prays, he doesn't forget to thank God for having allowed him to meet Mireille and making him look like this American actor.

Also telling himself that now we write each other so often and we make plans, we say to each other, tomorrow, when it's over, it'll be over soon. All that, at night. And that movement he hears, on his right, as if someone had just moved forward, walked. And now the cracking sound isn't coming from steps over branches or brush, no, what's cracking is only his teeth grinding in his mouth, fear in his mouth and his jaws clenched so hard it might make his gums bleed or break his teeth when the burst of gunfire comes to pierce the night—not far on his right, a flash of light, white, bluish, its blinding intensity and the echo invading the whole space and suddenly he's lying with his face on the ground and his hands ready to fire, his fingers tight on the trigger.

He's shaking. He's breathing hard. His whole body is shaking and the buzzing in his ears is so loud he can't hear his breath, or the cicadas, or the shouts of the guys further on. He doesn't know yet that the guy who fired only took fright at the shapes of three dogs bolting toward the base and prowling too near them; he doesn't know that two of the dogs are dead and another took to the hills and has already disappeared—all he knows is his jaw hurts and he can't stop his tears. There's this cracking in his throat, a tightening, like a burn, a vise, and his pants are soaked, his bladder is completely emptied and something in his head is distorting every muscle in his face so much it hurts.

And yet, when the next day comes, it'll be the same world, the same melody in the morning,

So-and-so! Java duty!

As if last night was nothing. They'll pretend it was nothing at all.

It'll be this one's or that one's turn to get up and bring the coffee from the kitchen. Sometimes it's his turn, but most often not, and so he does like everybody else, he grumbles along with the whole platoon, all twenty-five men. Transistors crackle out the first news of the day, voices yell for them to turn it off, turn it down, and with eyes still half-shut all of them go take a leak against the little wall outside, a bit further off.

Today, he'll write Solange. As he often does, to pass the time and ask how things are going, say he's stuffing himself with sausage, coffee, and jam here.

He can write this: things are okay.

He can also ask how the family is, what's happening to them—he doesn't dare write "back home," it's too sentimental and hypocritical and he insists she give him news of this one and that one, he wants her to report details, conversations, but also stories about what's going on in town and also news of other guys who left like him to defend peace with automatic rifles and boots and save the country. He hadn't really understood the country was in danger, since nothing ever happens and you're bored to death there.

And when he asks for news in his letters, it's not really because he wants to know how the brothers and sisters are doing—they're still sleeping in the bedrooms next to the parents' room, four together across the width of the bed, yes, he knows it, and four others in the room at the back, that makes eight, plus a few others sleeping somewhere else, at their bosses' place in the farmhouses around and also a few others lying in coffins for all eternity. And him here on an iron cot with an ash-gray blanket that serves as a bedspread, with cans filled with water under it so the vermin can drown in them.

At least he has his own bed. He's lucky, they keep repeating to him. Because here, the barracks are made of cinderblocks, while others are tents and tents let the fells' knife blades go through like butter they explain to him, and bullets still more easily.

Yes, it's good here.

He can write Solange that the situation could have been worse for him. We're not far from Oran, and he says he saw their cousin Rabut there and met Mireille with him and other people, too, Philibert, Gisèle, and Jacqueline.

He says they have assembly around eight and they stay at attention through the raising of the flag. That's when they look at the flag in the blue sky, when they try to convince themselves they're here for something like ideas, an ideal, some kind of higher goal, preserving civilization or something, like it said in one of the booklets he was given when he got here.

They give themselves missions, goals, and the base commander's mood is the barometer of the day. Maintenance work, weapons and barracks inspection, and instruction for the new recruits, target practice. They're stuck between the sea and the hills, they're here to protect the big oil tanks. They also protect the director of the refinery and his family. At the beginning they were surprised to see that an Algerian was appointed to this position, if the tanks are so important and oil such a precious commodity, how come it's an Algerian who's in charge, they wonder; they don't know there's also an Arab bourgeoisie.

Besides, they almost never see the man, and his wife still less. She stays at home, which is inside the base but still far enough from the center for them to feel apart from it. When you're on inspection or sentry duty you have to walk all the way behind the house, a stone house like in France, a simple cube with two floors, and go around it behind the little vegetable garden, up to the barbed wire. That makes the walk a lot longer, and they don't particularly like going that way because the distance from the rest of the base is sometimes a little unsettling, especially at night. It's a dark spot, you hold your rifle in your hands as you walk ahead and you lean forward to see better, on the alert.

Sometimes you can see the light through one of the windows.

He doesn't tell Solange that some men claim they've seen the shape of the wife naked behind the curtain, or even naked at the window. Nobody believes that, but once or twice everybody stayed a little longer than necessary under the window of the only civilians in the base, just to see if ever.

Except that no, never.

On the other hand, he can say they see the husband crossing the yard very early in the morning and heading to his office on the other side of the base, in a prefabricated building where he works. No one really understands what he does there all day. They know he has visitors, and trucks come in regularly, accompanied by a platoon just for the trucks alone, so great is the fear of attacks. The trucks are filled up, then they leave again.

Sometimes one can see the couple's little girl, too. She's always dressed in dark clothes. Bernard walks by her often when he's inspecting the base, with Février, Nivelle, Poiret, or someone else.

When you walk near their house, you can sometimes hear the cries of a newborn baby.

The little girl is shy, or she's scared, they don't know which. Whatever the reason, when they ask her name or how old she is, she lowers her eyes when she answers. Fatiha, that's the name she whispers.

Fatiha is eight.

And then lunch and the afternoon nap. Strange, long days, like the ones he knows with the cows in the fields, when the only music you get is the buzzing of the flies and your own breath, heavy, panting, in the hollow of an afternoon nap.

But here, it's different. He's not the only one who's alone, all of them are alone together.

This afternoon, he's not the only one who doesn't feel like talking.

They walk on without saying anything. They listen to the cicadas and the crunch of loose stones rolling under their feet, they just walk following the guy ahead, without knowing where they're going, without waiting either. They listen to Nivelle talk about the peasants here, pitying them because with soil like that, nothing must grow, he says. And then Abdelmalik answers no, he remembers that here, before, there used to be wheat, they grew wheat but the peasants in the relocation centers can't work the land anymore.

You call that land?

Yes. There used to be wheat, before.

And they also talk about the gigantic olive trees whose green color is almost gray, they've never seen that back home; everything is so white here, or milky, without shadow, without depth, even the hills melt into the sky, even the blue isn't blue but seems diluted in a whitish mist where mountain and sky fuse together. That's something you have time to see. Because you never come across anybody. You don't see anybody. Only stones, dust, flies landing on the sweat of their faces and sticking to it; and their eyes already squinting to see what's ahead, a hundred meters away, a pile of stones, constructions, the shapes of a small village.

From far off, yes, it looks like a village.

A few low walls and scattered, spindly tufts of yellow, stringy crabgrass where families and houses used to be. Bernard doesn't understand why the people were sent away but gets the feeling it's better not to ask. They walk silently through the little paths that used to be narrow streets, perhaps.

Sometimes you can see a whole set of furniture made of clay. Sometimes the things are sculpted and the set has been decorated, or only parts, big drawings, often of snakes.

They're going to leave, they can't stay here, as if it were a cemetery. Bernard thinks of what he's been told about Oradour-sur-Glane, and that thought makes him thirsty for a few seconds, a strange kind of thirst that must be quenched right away, but the others have already started moving; for a few seconds he just stands there, lost in space, his eyes staring at a shattered earthenware jar in what might have been a kitchen.

Afterward, when they're at the relocation center, they have to walk through the camp, inspect it, and today Bernard looks at the people and wonders what they would do, what we would do, in the hamlets of La Migne, if soldiers had come in and razed everything, broke everything, prevented us from farming, from working.

He imagines.

All those people out of work that soldiers would be herding into some relocation center. He imagines and wonders if they, too, would do what the men in the camp do, laying out plastic basins on the ground, turning themselves into grocers or hardware merchants just because they have two or three basins to sell, or drivers with a license in their pockets but no car, or, why not, carpenters with some old rusty nails in a chicory can, would that be enough to bear the humiliation of being out of work, could the men he knows bear being moved away from their crops and see barbed wire around their children?

You see men in woolen djellabas who sit there for hours on end without talking.

Like big bags.

You'd think they were bags of cement because they don't move, waiting for what, Bernard doesn't know; he just imagines what it would be like for the men back home to experience the same humiliation, for a farmer to be deprived of what gives him his reason for living. He imagines his brothers and the children playing the way he's seen the children here, around the fountain, with toys made out of steel wire—wheels as thin as twigs, carts as fragile as paper, and the eyes of two sisters, one wearing braids and the other in a pink dress with light blue swallows on it and gold thread to emphasize the design.

They look at the people attentively. He's not sure why he looks at the people the way he does, at their wretched poverty, as if he'd never seen that before, but he's so tired, and angry too, what the hell are we doing here, he can see it's ridiculous, being here makes no sense, let's go home, let's leave the faces you see here with what scares you in them, their silence, their seriousness, their shining eyes, is it fever, is it anger?

You don't know.

And you don't know why, but you know you're scared. And in Bernard's mouth there is the same taste as last night, but weaker, more persistent; the people look at the soldiers and they, the soldiers, walk between the shacks, slowly, very slowly, and he's one of the soldiers, one of the young men, so young, walking along the paths.

He walks calmly and inside himself he finds this camp absurd, laid out in a straight line that way, with its town hall, its fountain and its wretched poverty, its undernourished children with dirty hair, the astonished eyes they have when you finally walk in and search their place without asking them anything, without them daring to do anything against us.

Because in the camp there's always that same appearance of calm and resigned peace; the same violence in the bright eyes of the women, the babies with their eyes shut and their bellies swollen like balloons; and then the men who sit there without saying anything, waiting.

Tomorrow, some of the men will leave for Oran. Bernard isn't one of them and will have to stay at the base.

He'll have to stay there all day and wait for the others to return, spend his afternoon imagining the missed opportunity. He doesn't feel like talking cars with Nivelle. It's a very hot, very heavy day, but the presence of the sea promises some coolness. He takes a nap and walks around the base for part of the afternoon, partly out of boredom or to stretch his legs; that's the day he comes upon little Fatiha sitting in the shade of an olive tree.

She's playing and doesn't see him right away. When she raises her eyes to him, he smiles at her and asks what she's playing. He walks over and she—in a voice that's not loud but sure of itself, like the voice of what a child of eight can imagine a grown-up's voice should sound like—she spontaneously gives him a lesson, you take some olives, not ripe ones but not too hard either, and you throw them like this (at that moment she throws the two olives she's holding in her hand), there, then you turn over your hand, they have to fall on the back of your hand, and if you miss your opponent hits the back of your hand with his fingers, like this, one hit for each olive you missed, see, I missed one, you have to hit me with your finger.

And so he kneels down with the child and both of them play for a few minutes, and soon both of them get caught up in the game. Bernard throws and can't always catch the olives. He enjoys Fatiha's seriousness as she puts her fingers together and hits the back of his hand, loudly counting the number of times she hits him.

He wants to suggest something too, he has an idea and he likes that idea so much that suddenly he smiles and asks if Fatiha would like to come along with him. She hesitates, thinks for a bit, then answers that her mother doesn't really like her to talk to soldiers but okay, yes, a little secret, her mother won't know.

When they get to the barracks, it's not empty, three or four men are there, Poiret and Nivelle among them. Bernard and Fatiha go over to a box that has a turtle in it.

It's our mascot. They're the ones who found it.

A turtle, I didn't know there were turtles.

No, we didn't either.

And now Nivelle and Poiret also walk over to the box and look at the animal. Poiret picks it up carefully, you see that the turtle's paws are like the limbs of a swimmer doing the breaststroke in slow motion and seen from underneath; Fatiha shrinks back for a second, the time to get scared, to scare herself, to laugh too, astonished, taken aback, and finally Poiret holds out the turtle to her, asking her to be careful, its teeth are sharp and the little nails on its paws are very sharp, too.

Fatiha asks if she can come back, the men say yes, whenever she wants.

When she leaves, Bernard walks her back. He's walking next to her when she starts to run to get back to her scooter: she left it near the trucks, well before her house.

He'll still have to wait. Wait for the others to return from Oran.

Bernard is disappointed not to have gone with them, because every time the city is like a breath of fresh air. Wait some more for the men who'll have something to tell and bring back the mail they're all hoping for.

He remembers the first time he went to Oran, the half-track in the lead and the jeep tracing the way, and also that nobody was thinking about the risk of an ambush but only of those few hours they would have given anything for, because after you got the supplies at the CP, you knew you'd be spending the afternoon in the streets, the cafés, you'd go listen to music, who knows, nothing seems impossible when for once you know you'll be far from those big gray oil reservoirs that close off the horizon on one side and on the other, their counterpart, the hills.

There are several of them walking through the city together, looking at the shop windows, the palm trees—you have glimpses of the sea and you hear the noise of traffic, you don't know yet how banal and clichéd the extraordinary images of the veiled women are. Women on scooters. That one, who drives by wrapped up in surprisingly white veils, they can see her eyes looking straight ahead of her and her brows furrowed, and this detail which amuses them: yellow plastic shoes with high heels.

It amuses them or it doesn't. It stirs them too, surprises them. It brings their minds back to the idea of going to see women, and they know where to go.

As for him, he hadn't followed the others, that, too, he remembers, he remembers his cousin Rabut; they had arranged to meet in the Choupot neighborhood, but first he remembers the walk through the city with Idir, surprised to walk through the city with an Algerian, in silence, one guiding the other without talking to him, without either of them even trying to say anything—it doesn't occur to them to ask each other questions, they don't think of it, each is going to do what he has to do. Bernard knows Idir's going to meet his family, that's enough for him. He doesn't know that Idir enlisted in the army to defend France like his grandfather, the family hero, decorated, honored, with one of his arms left behind in the mud of Verdun.

Bernard doesn't ask him anything, they simply walk and look at the city.

On some walls you can read,

Algeria will win. Free Algeria.

The graffiti have been scratched out, scraped, they've been vaguely painted over but along the shape of the letters, so they remain legible. They act as if they hadn't seen them, but something of those graffiti remains in the sounds of the city and the silence between the two men, like a doubt, an uncertainty: for Bernard, a vague fear, a kind of premonition.

He thinks that among the men and women they pass on the street some of them want him dead, him and all the others wearing the uniform of the army.

But at the same time all of this seems fake to him because there's the sun and the city, you hear conversations about nothing, laughter, life, the beat of a whole city, the noise of engines—cars and scooters—a man sitting in front of his little butcher shop watching children play soccer on a little square, barefoot, with a can rolling around with a frightful noise and sometimes stopping silently in the schoolbags and sweaters that serve as a net.

Is that what war is like?

Then he can see the afternoon with Rabut again, and how Rabut talks about taking lots of pictures—the army newspaper, *Le Bled*, you know, *Le Bled*, organized a contest, and he says he won a Kodak. Ever since, he's been snapping the guys and the landscapes when they go out, and he takes pictures of veiled women and the people in the markets. But most often from behind, because they don't really like you to take their picture.

He also recalls his first meeting with Mireille, the guys all very high on the way back, they'd had a few, they saw women and they make fun of him a little,

So, had a good time with your cousin?

And he looks at his buddies without laughing. He's even shocked that Février went to the women, too. And in Bernard's silence and unforgiving look, Février senses what he blames him for: Éliane.

Février shrugs to say that has nothing to do with it, he knows very well that has nothing to do with it. And besides he confides to Bernard that going with a prostitute isn't really cheating and what he did is even less cheating; and almost whispering, getting slightly closer to his ear, he tells him he didn't sleep with the girl, even if he went up to her room he didn't sleep with her, he just unbuckled his belt, lowered his pants, and stayed there standing with his eyes shut, drawing the girl's head to him and letting his hands slide in her hair to go along with her motion.

That's all, it's not really cheating.

When they return at the end of the afternoon, the men in the convoy bring back the mail. Février is not in a good mood at all, Bernard can tell right away; he can feel his friend's animosity, his anger or disappointment: he didn't get a letter, Éliane hasn't written in two weeks.

What Bernard doesn't know yet, at the time he gets a letter from Mireille, is that he soon will be bitterly disappointed too, almost furious. He doesn't know this. Not yet. For the moment he's holding the envelope in his hands, his fingers are shaking, his whole being is shaking and it seems to him that happiness is written all over his cheeks, his forehead, his eyes.

But that won't last.

Not that Mireille's telling him anything whose tone or feeling could give him something to worry about. On the contrary, the letter is very long, she talks about being eager to see him again and even suggests a few things they might do together. But what she says in passing, as if for him it wouldn't be important at all and in any case it wasn't for her, is that often, well no, let's say not often, a few times, once in a café and two other times in a nightclub open in the afternoon, she's seen his cousin Rabut.

She says he's *adorable*; Bernard doesn't yet know how much scorn and repugnance he feels for this word, because he doesn't know, at this point, how a word can be contemptible and cowardly as much as a cousin, let's say, that particular cousin—Rabut. And Bernard only has time to brood over his rage and, for the first time, to feel a kind of anger at Mireille, a kind of resentment at the naiveté of her words and the thoughtlessness of her conduct.

So, because the jealousy he feels is a shameful emotion, he doesn't talk about it.

He spends part of the evening with the other men, playing cards in the rec hall before dinner. When he stops playing and joins Février at a table, he almost feels relieved; it's as if he wasn't thinking about anything.

But Février, on the other hand, is not thinking of nothing. He drinks his beer and asks Bernard if he doesn't want to get out of here, too much noise. Outside they walk slowly, the time for Février to talk of his disappointment when he looked inside the mailbag and realized that this time, too, he wouldn't have a letter, none, not even from his parents but okay, they can't write, and his brothers and sisters could write too, but no, and Éliane.

Except she.

Like a stomach cramp, a heart cramp. It's so unfair and still, again, the dumb hope you hang on to, whereas Février and Bernard both know what Éliane doesn't want to say, and what she means by not sending any more letters.

And then, with a laugh, Février says that today again we went to see women, him and the guys. Not the same one he saw last time. He says,

Another one, prettier, a blonde with huge breasts, you should've seen her. This time I really felt like laying her down on the bed and touching her breasts, that really turns me on.

And he laughs. Bernard starts laughing too.

All's fair in love and war, that's what they say, right?

Well no.

I just did like the other time, I thought of Éliane and I told myself it couldn't possibly be over, not like that, I don't believe it, no, she can't do that to me.

So?

So I dropped my pants and just stood there like I was at attention.

And they both laugh because of the absurd, incongruous image. Then they're quiet, and Février doesn't say how he feels like crying and the effort he's making not to show it.

And then, there's that doctor who came with them from Oran, and the medical examination where everyone goes on about how hungry and fed up they are, getting the same food all the time, not terrible, but so much always the same. He hears the same words everywhere, on all the bases, the doctor says, as if that should reassure or mollify them to learn that others share the same problems. The doctor says there's nothing he can do, but they feel, through his perplexed look, that he understands them, yes, men so young should be eating more.

And on the way out from his checkup Bernard sees them. Idir and Châtel in the yard: Idir, furious, provoking Châtel and giving him little finger-slaps that turn into real slaps, always on the same spot, slaps which suddenly resound and punctuate the same words,

What is it, what d'you mean? What d'you want from me?

And at first Châtel smiles and doesn't think the other guy is serious; then his smile freezes when he realizes Idir isn't joking and he turns very pale, he doesn't answer, or just vaguely, nothing, in a shaky voice almost as expressionless as his face, and the dust rises in the shuffle.

At first the others hesitate. Some of them think of separating them. Then others say,

No, let's have some laughs.

They laugh all right, and they begin to make bets, two or three cigarettes, they form a circle in the yard, and the circle tightens around them, they yell and Idir's getting increasingly furious because he can sense that Châtel is refusing to fight and he doesn't want to hit him. Idir thinks it's cowardice, Châtel is a coward, that's all, and he starts to curse him out because a man who challenges another should be ready to fight, to defend himself, not like Châtel, who hints at things without taking responsibility for them.

Bernard walks over, asks Nivelle why they're going to fight.

Because Châtel said that what they're doing here is disgusting and the *harkis* are betraying the Algerians. The other guy didn't like it. He said his family has to eat and the army is a job like any other job and he's just as French as anybody else.

So they're going to fight.

Except that Châtel doesn't really understand what's happening and he remains inert, hardly stirred by the punches in his shoulder, his body swaying with every punch, his hips, his legs, his feet going with the shock and pivoting slightly backward then coming back, straightening up and moving in an increasingly wide arc. The other men laugh at first, and then, as he doesn't react, curse him out, call him a wimp, a faggot, come on, hit him one. And Châtel more and more livid looks around for someone in the crowd who could help him, save him, understand him, explain why he's there, now, and why he's going to get hit, why an Algerian's going to hit him, since he's always defending the Algerians. He doesn't get it. To tell the truth, he'd like to just say he's sorry, say he didn't mean to be insulting. But the other men are pushing him to strike back. So he throws a few clumsy, soft punches, as if fatigue were preventing him from aiming, as if he had no strength in his arms.

The corporal has walked over and nobody pays any attention to him. He looks at the scene without saying anything. Idir throws a punch, one punch, one single punch and Châtel collapses, then tries to get up and falls down again under the shouts, the laughs, they're having fun, he makes them laugh and instead of getting mad Châtel feels something collapsing in his chest and the words and laughs lacerate him as well as the punches, they tell him to get up, to fight, and he tries, he tries, he'd like to keep trying, but everything in him refuses, his body doesn't want to, he knows it but he'd like to fight against himself, too.

The corporal walks into the circle and asks who started it. Idir defends himself, he says the other insulted him, he said that—

And then he falls silent, he refuses to speak.

Châtel gets up and looks by turns at the corporal, Idir, and the other guys around them. He says he's sorry. He swears he didn't mean to insult Idir, something Idir refuses to believe— but the corporal's voice cuts in to interrupt everything, you're even, that's enough. All the men here are French and they're all under his command.

The next day, the incident that overshadows the whole day isn't Châtel's fight or what each man has retained of the corporal's words. As if suddenly all that belonged to another time, far away. Because the corporal's voice won't be that forceful when he gives them the news, in the yard where they've all been summoned, that the doctor was kidnapped on his way back to Oran. There's talk of an ambush. There's talk of shots and they are told that a car has fallen into the hands of the fells.

The car was found with two gendarmes in it. Their throats were cut. The doctor was not in the jeep.

And the feeling of helplessness gets even stronger when they learn it's men from another platoon who will be interrogating the people in the camp, and also that men from the Foreign Legion will be searching the hills. You tell yourself you can't do anything, for a moment you feel negligible and useless.

You don't realize that this time around you've been spared a nasty job.

You feel angry, and in the evening, when it's time to go to the rec hall, you can feel that anger in your pockets as you empty them a little more frantically than usual, to look for a cigarette but mostly for change to buy a beer. They crowd around the bar, this evening maybe more than any other. They'll drink beer, nobody will play foosball. And even the card games will be played without a shout, without a laugh.

One more silence.

And when Février walks into the barracks with his beer in his hand, he stands there disconcerted for a moment: Bernard and Châtel are sitting next to each other, each with his hands clasped, their heads bowed, their eyes closed. They hardly move when he walks in. But he stays there, he doesn't leave. He's embarrassed, certainly, but he understands.

They'll only talk about it afterward.

He says: Prayers won't help the doc.

Maybe it can help us?

You believe that, Bernard? You really believe that?

I don't know. I know it helps me.

Yeah, but how about the doc?

And when Châtel wants to speak, he doesn't have the time to open his mouth or even move, Février doesn't leave him the time,

141

Yeah, go say that to his wife, go tell her we're a bunch of ass-holes, right, you go tell her. Go tell her that.

Châtel doesn't answer.

He stays like that, frozen, his eyes fixed on Février, because it's the first time he's heard him talk in this tone, with such violence. Trembling slightly too, imperceptibly, it's like a vibration, fear barely hidden by the movement of his hand raising the bottle to his mouth; and the sound of the beer when it reaches the neck of the bottle, then a mouthful of beer and for a second you hear him swallowing and the silence right after that, but fear is in the air, in the sudden way Février has of catching his breath, and it's the same for Bernard and Châtel.

And then Février starts smiling again; he holds up the bottle, Hey, guys, to each his own God, after all.

And now things are different. In the calm of the night, it's not peace and soothing coolness you feel, it's fear, fear creeps in, very slowly at first, because they're thinking of the doctor, of the two gendarmes who were found slaughtered; and you try not to tell yourself it could have been you, you can see them leaving on the path in the afternoon and you know their vigilance and their weapons within arm's reach were useless. It's mostly at night that you think about it, but you don't tell anyone. Because if you did, you'd have to say why you have diarrhea, why the stomach cramps and the loss of appetite, why you drink liters of water and you're still thirsty.

A few days later there's that body they find not far from the spot where that same day, just a few hours earlier, they discovered telephone poles which had been sawed down.

They tell themselves,

That's why the fells cut down the telephone poles. Because they knew someone would come to repair them and would find the body before it was devoured by the animals, the jackals and stray dogs, before the sun wreaked havoc on it, burned it up, made it unrecognizable, so it would still be sufficiently intact, you could say *legible,* yes, so everybody could really understand what was said here, what is being said through it. That's why the fells sawed down the poles. So someone would come back and they could leave a corpse there without running the risk of being found or located, with nobody around.

That's what they think, anyway.

And they see the men who've come back to notify the base. The guys who went to repair the telephone poles and the guys who went with them for protection. They had radioed first. And the men pile into the medical half-track, Nivelle and Bernard among them, with their rifles on their shoulders, with no other news, without really knowing what they'll find where they're going. Even if they tell themselves. And imagine. Because the nurse is with them; they're riding in the ambulance. And the dust on the trail. The wind clacking on the metal of the car and the canvas top with the red cross painted on it, the sand like iron filings, the bumpy trail, the coughing engine, its loud rumblings and vibrations under their feet through the floor, and the men holding their breath, already; they look straight ahead and also along the sides at the line of olive trees in the distance, they know the wadi's there down below, that road they know now, and the fear they feel rising inside themselves, they already know it, too.

Then they get to the meeting point. Others come out to meet them, they see a jeep and the radio operator.

They hear the captain's voice, he's getting irritated and he's hanging on to the handset of the transmitter,

Negative! Negative!

And they don't understand. There are men there smoking and looking at the ground a little further on, at first they don't notice how pale they all are; with them there's an Arab in a djellaba. With his handset still in his hand, the captain suddenly stops talking, then looks at them:

He's yours.

He points to the mass whose shape they see at the foot of an embankment near one of the poles that was sawed off at the base and is leaning into the air, not down completely yet.

They already know it's a body. And Bernard wonders, is he going to see a man with his throat cut? Bernard thinks again about all the stories you hear in France—stories he heard echoes of back home, at the market on Sundays—when they talk of terribly mutilated bodies, of that appalling sight you tried to imagine without ever really succeeding. And he looks a few meters further on over there, next to the embankment, at that shape. First he can't make out the body but only the bare feet of the man, dirty feet whitened by the dust, like his pants. He tells himself the men who killed him kept his shoes.

They walk forward slowly. They start talking again, then they fall silent, they clear their throats and exchange glances, yes, we're coming—the body is in a strange position they don't understand right away, as if it were sideways, its right arm hidden and its head in profile, leaning back, as if the chin were completely thrust forward offering up its throat—but the throat is not sliced open, you can see the gaping mouth and the eyes very black already, sunk into the dark sockets, swollen, and the hair almost gray because of the dust, and all that sand in the hair, on the tight skin, that strange, almost broken color of the skin, too, not yet hardened, not yet totally burned because there is

144

still, under the skin and the shape of the skull, a face, and features they can recognize, almost, hardly, it will soon be over but it's still there, a human being, more or less, soon to give birth to a carcass, that's what Bernard tells himself, thinks, imagines—that face in profile where the cheek, like a hole, could open a second mouth, and the shirt whose collar is buttoned up to the neck; the hand and the left arm thrust behind let a sheet of paper float on the chest in front, pinned on with a safety pin, the bottom of the paper moving slightly, yes, stirring, almost nothing, and then they look more closely at the pants covered with stains, the stench already atrocious, the stains, and you understand what must have happened. The nurse walks over to the body, walks around it and gets to the level of the torso. There, he leans over, then hesitates, and says,

No.

He repeats to himself, in a whisper,

No,

Straightens up, looks at the others and,

Oh God. God, Jesus,

His face suddenly livid, he turns to the corpse anyway and rips off the paper; he walks back to the others to show them.

At first, what they see is a picture. They get the fells' idea. They're going to post it everywhere, they'll use it for propaganda.

French soldiers, your families are thinking of you, go home.

Bernard doesn't look at the picture, he walks toward the body, he wants to see, now, he wants to know and the first thing he wants to see is if the body has been mutilated at the throat. The throat is intact. You can see the bristles of a few days without shaving, the glottis and the very tight skin.

Bernard stays like that for a moment, he's surprised there's no blood on the throat. He refuses to see what will stare him in the face later on, because he hadn't been told that this, too, was possible.

On the way back, they cannot yet accept what they saw. And it's not the sand, not the desolation, not even the relative coolness of the morning and the nauseous heaves they're all going to have, one after the other, never at the same time, as if the time to react was different for each of them—none of this will change something of, how to call it, they don't know what to call what they see when they finally make up their minds to move the body and turn it on its back.

And afterward, at the base, for those who haven't seen, they'll just talk about the dust and the silence, about the flies already attacking the body and they'll pile up details, all the details they can think of to dress up the story in order to delay the moment they'll have to show and tell. The others, in the mess hall, will be very quick to understand that something's being kept from them, the truth, not the death of the doctor exactly, not even that his death is recent, yesterday probably, or this morning, but then how to tell guys who're waiting, incredulous but not yet mad just curious, with that slight fear or apprehension that keeps them alert and tense in their curiosity, not yet shaken and revolted as they'll become, afterward, when they find out.

To tell them: he was alive when they did that to him.

They did that to a living man, they cut through the flesh, the muscles. Everything, down to the bone. They scraped from the wrist all the way up to the shoulder. And you tell yourself that the man saw the skeleton of his arm. Scraped off. Ripped off. He fainted every time, the pain, you know, and those men, the ones who did that, with what, knives, knives that scrape, and him screaming and them, always waking him up, patiently, relentlessly, without pity, each time, until he understands that not only will they chop up his arm but they will rip out the muscles, and the flesh, down to the skeleton.

And why that precision, stopping at the wrist and the same precision at the level of the shoulder.

Death came but only at the last minute, on the road perhaps, very close to the spot where the corpse was found.

In the photograph you see him alive, his arm already half ripped apart, streaming blood, in the picture you can easily recognize the doctor despite the pain, with his eyes turned up, his mouth open, standing up, hanging by ropes under his armpits. And these words in big letters under the picture, words that will always come back to them:

French soldiers, your families are thinking of you, go home.

And then the way everything speeds up, the way something is happening very quickly because they set up a funerary chapel in the infirmary, and how all the men want to see because they refuse to tell themselves that such a thing is possible. And how that same evening in the rec hall, they all crowd around the bar—Bernard, like the others, searches his pockets for change to buy a beer and more cigarettes. With Nivelle, who hasn't said a word all day. And others, too. Châtel hasn't left the barracks, he's praying. Maybe he's crying and he's just afraid of meeting the others, all the others, who won't fail to ask him what he thinks now about the war of liberation. And he doesn't want to go back on what he said. He doesn't want to run into Février or speak to him, him or anyone else, it doesn't matter who, because he's not sure he thinks anything at all anymore.

He wonders if a cause can be just and its means, unjust. How is it possible to think that terror will lead to more good. He wonders if the good.

He doesn't want to go out and prefers to stay there alone and pray. He's surprised that Bernard doesn't want to pray with him. Bernard will only pray later, alone, when night has come, when in the silence of the barracks he will try to forget what he saw. He'll try. Just as in the rec hall, he tries not to interpret an exchange of looks he catches between Idir and Abdelmalik, apparently the conclusion of an argument which had been going on for some time, and even some kind of provocation directed at Idir, coming from Abdelmalik. Because both of them must tighten their jaws and keep quiet when they hear the guys talking about the Arabs, saying dogs, all of them are dogs, nothing but dogs all of them—and they're not talking about the fells when they use those words, no, they're talking about Arabs, as if all Arabs, as if.

And the two *harkis* say nothing. They wait. They watch.

As if they were the only ones who hadn't forgotten where they were born.

Early next morning there's total pandemonium. It's the first time Bernard has seen so many people at the base.

Reinforcements got there early, at dawn. Among them, Bernard recognizes Rabut and some other guys stationed in Oran. There are several platoons. They're going to comb the sector, they stay like that in the morning for almost an hour, it's not clear yet what kind of action will be taken, if any. For the first time at the base there's something different from the usual slowness, something other than the boredom that has been weighing on you for weeks on end, on your morale, your intelligence, your body, as if every day you've been getting number and number while others, out there in the hills, cut your friends' throats and dismember them.

So this time, from the way they're preparing, he can feel a kind of energy and anger at the base; it even seems to him that this morning none of them watched the flag go up in the same way they do every day—this time in the blue sky there's something like an urge to go out and run, yell, say they want to get it over with and some of them think that once they're in the hills, once they've been in combat they'll be soldiers, too, soldiers who've been under fire and they can go home and take up their normal lives again in the fields and factories. And not be afraid anymore. Not have stomachaches, not be hungry, hungry so often, not so often feel the urge to leave those stinking latrines behind, and that rancid odor of sweat in the barracks. And Châtel with his prayers and clasped hands, Bernard with his missal, his postcard of the phosphorescent Virgin over his bed, and the others, each one with his own quirks, his stories, and all the cockroaches and vermin that circulate among us, the fleas, the bedbugs, no matter how hard you scrub yourself, and the same endless days, we tell ourselves,

This time we'll finish tearing up our last pairs of socks, already so worn out in the boots with our toes bleeding inside them even when we're not marching, our feet will bleed on the stony trails once and for all and afterward, after that, maybe it'll be all over and instead of a four-day furlough for the fourteenth of July they'll tell us,

It's over, you can go home and thank you very much peace has returned to Algeria,

Just because some old rifles from the First World War were dug out of holes and they found some guys as skinny as death hiding in improbable caves, with feverish eyes shining like Christmas candles.

And it'll be over.

That's what they tell themselves, what they're waiting for. It'll be over. That's how they set out, all of them, and they end up hoping for the horrible march with swollen toes, cracked heels or the skin bursting like a translucent bubble, bubbles, blisters and oozing pus, blackened nails ready to fall off, with blood underneath. They want to go for it. Even if they know it's going to be hot and they'll be walking single file carrying a whole hardware supply of explosive and smoke grenades—and woe to whoever hangs back, the stragglers stumbling along, the soles of their feet rolling over the stones, under the weight of their bags, their cartridge belts, their rifles, and there won't be a single one of them thinking of going home but all of them will find the energy to march in the sun and tell themselves,

It's the humiliation, that's right,

You can't do this you can't do that my ass: punishments rain down on us like the plague of frogs in the bible, the stupid chores, the bullying, the endless pushups, the constant orders and laps around the yard with your rifle over your head and the bolt between your teeth, and the huge, gluey garbage cans without handles from the mess hall, the garbage, our shit, our rubbish, the meals, swill, dried-out meat, leather soles, moldy bread and all the maggots, cans, mush, and the potatoes and the beans, the whole load of it oozing out of obese garbage cans, and dragging them, sliding them along slowly without throwing up because of the stench, without knocking them down, rolling them up to the truck—you might find some compassionate soul, a seminarian, a greenhorn, a student, a city guy, all those white hands to get rid of that shit without having to negotiate, that crap or some other, our ass out in the *djebels* looking for an enemy and finally finding one, anyone, deserters, fells, bandits, men, women, shadows, a jackal or a horse or just something moving in the brush, something with a little more consistency than a nightmare under the shrubs and the crawling vegetation,

That's what we want, let's get it all over with.

The decision has been made to leave the jeeps and half-tracks near the wadi. They'll keep going on foot. Some of them will stay here, and Bernard and Idir are among the few guys who'll wait for the two platoons to return.

They watch the others leave between the rocks. Bernard won't know what's going to happen, or he'll picture the bayonets opening the crumbly earth to find the entrances to arms caches, the men looking at the ground, probing the earth and the clumps of shrubs for hours. And since they don't find anything they walk deeper into the rocks, already frustrated, humiliated at the prospect of returning empty-handed from a hunt in which they don't even know what they're hunting.

You have to go far to find more than razed villages deserted by their inhabitants in order to come upon signs of human presence that are not cans of mackerel in white wine sauce in the dust and the stones. So you have to keep walking and sometimes you hear the buzzing of a Piper Cub high above you, no bigger than a toy, and its shadow is like the shadow of a stubborn, rigid bird that keeps coming back to guide us, to help us, over the same pieces of blackened branches, already burning hot. But there's nothing but thirsty clumps of plants looking for water just as we're looking for the fells, the rifles, the caches, and so we readjust the blue scarf that identifies us on our left shoulder, because we're pretty sure the only people we're likely to run into are our own people, but you never know, we don't want to fire at each other.

And in the distance you look for something that will make you think it's worth keeping on, bearing the heat and the buzzing plane and the big circles it sometimes traces over your head when it stays up there too long—and that exasperation, too, when you're faced with always the same palm trees and their green head of hair, and the very tall, scaly trunks of the date trees, the oleanders everywhere, indestructible, that crap you thought was so beautiful at the beginning, and that very blue sky, the blue of the infinite monotony of postcards, the bees too, sometimes, and the flies, always.

And when they finally reach a village, they deploy so as to encircle it, and hearts are beating this time because here the village is not deserted: they have walked so far that the forbidden, uninhabitable zone has been left behind a long time ago.

And then, when they see us, the inhabitants must hesitate, incredulous before the men who come running up to their houses with guns in their hands—a woman remains there in the middle, in front of them, with wicker branches on her head that she's maintaining with one hand, and she stands there dumfounded, it takes some time before she understands, before she realizes, and then she turns around as if nothing were happening.

Soon she disappears behind a door.

And Bernard and Idir are sitting next to each other in the shade of the jeeps. At first they don't talk. Then Bernard says he shouldn't take it personally, what the guys are saying about the Arabs, it's because they're scared and angry.

Idir can understand that, he doesn't bear a grudge against anybody. He says,

You think Kabyles are Arabs. For you, all Algerians are the same. I'm not an Arab, I'm a Berber.

Bernard doesn't know what to answer, after all he can't even recognize an accent from Marseilles. He'd like to say that to defend himself, but he just nods. He'd like to talk about Abdelmalik, who's with the others, but he doesn't dare.

Idir's the one who speaks.

Abdelmalik, it really bugs him when they talk like that about Arabs, he says we'll never be French. Whatever we do. He says the people here, we're fighting them, it's war and we call it peace.

He doesn't look at Bernard when he speaks. He shakes a stick around in front of him and draws incomprehensible figures in the sand.

And then the others will be back and they'll start marching again.

They'll march for hours, without daring to ask what happened in the village — they have a pretty good idea, they heard shooting, and black smoke went through the sky with the smell of burning straw. Nivelle has no qualms telling how where he was stationed before, with other guys, in the South,

Oh man, we really showed 'em.

And he remembers a guy who'd cut off the fells' ears and gave them to the woman who sold him cigarettes at the tobacco shop —

Nivelle, shut the fuck up, that's enough.

They set up camp.

And if you're afraid of sleeping in canvas tents, you're even more afraid of being ordered to guard the improvised camp.

What they don't know yet is how, when they fall asleep almost despite themselves, they'll wake up with a start because they hear artillery firing in the night. They look at each other, first they're not sure and they realize only at the second round that it's going to last for hours, the bombardment will last a long time, a very long time, and they understand why camp was set up here, so near a village, to shell it, that's right, and sleep won't come, you won't get used to it, your body will jump with every blast and your ears are ringing already.

They look at each other. They get out of the tents to see. It's night and sometimes you see bursts of light, the earth rumbles, it reverberates under your feet: a vibration that gets into your bones and ears.

There are fells over there.

Someone's yelling, repeating,

There are fells.

The guy next to Bernard says there must be fells, otherwise they wouldn't fire, there are fells and that way there won't be hand-to-hand combat and that's a good thing, that's what he says, what he's repeating, and Bernard hears the guy's voice, his shaky voice that doesn't believe what it's saying, his eyes shining in the night.

And the next morning they get up with aching bodies, stiff muscles, it's dawn, very early. Everywhere there is the smell of gunpowder in the air and that silence when they have to walk through the grayness of dawn, all the way over there, to that village you can't see for the moment except for a dark shape diluted in the black smoke—the smell already, even from far off, the smell of ashes, they don't dare tell themselves yet but they think of burned flesh, of smells they do not yet know.

The next day is a day of great fatigue and silence at the base.

A day when Rabut is there among the reinforcements. He has to leave the same evening, he and the others. In a few hours the base will return to what it was before. Then it will be the fourteenth of July, and some guys will get a furlough in Oran for three or four days.

But meanwhile they stay there, it lasts for a few strange hours, very long, interminable. They wait for all the platoons to meet there so they can all go back together. Bernard pretends he doesn't know what Mireille confided to him in her letters, that she saw Rabut at least two or three times, and danced with him twice, in the afternoon, in a club. He wonders what Rabut's doing here, he can't wait for him to leave with his whole company. He can't wait to get back to the calm and even the boredom and lethargy, to the way it was before. He'd like to doze away and wait, calmly, quietly, for the time of his leave in Oran.

He already wrote Mireille to tell her he'd be there for four days.

Soon the base fills up with all the platoons. They had never seen that many men there before, especially in the rec hall. No weapons had been found. No *fellaghas* either.

And yet they have the feeling they've been in combat, they've experienced something that feels like war, but above all they feel great fatigue, the urge to take off their boots, to take care of their feet that hurt horribly, have a beer, sleep. They'll play cards and try to think of something else; because they're also eager to hear that the doctor's body is far away from them.

They'd like it all to be over.

As always, Bernard and Rabut stay together, sitting beside each other on the steps of the rec hall. They don't talk about anything. Bernard doesn't say anything. Nothing about the hours he spent chewing over his anger and reading the words over and over where Mireille talks about the nightclub with that unbearable word for Rabut: *adorable*. He doesn't say any of that and doesn't ask his cousin anything either, if he's still engaged to Nicole, if he has news of the family.

And he could even ask about Mireille. But no, he doesn't do it; he thinks it's better not to show he's thinking about that.

The two cousins walk around the base for a few hours during the afternoon; they talk with the mechanics about the engines of the jeeps and about the trucks they'll have to check out soon. They also look at the helicopter in front of the entrance to the base. Rabut disappears for a few minutes, and when he comes back he has his camera in his hands. He can't take many pictures because he has almost no film left. But a few nonetheless, here, at the base. He says he'll send them to Solange and the family,

I'm sure nobody has a picture of you, back home.

Bernard doesn't answer, he's thinking of the bodies in the village they shelled all night—women and children, dogs too, a donkey and a few goats. He can hear the captain's voice yelling in the morning for them to find the weapons and the fells, and all of them work away furiously, lifting up stones, ashes, dust. There's nothing but death—and the stupid face of the captain spitting and not understanding and yelling like a madman for them to find those fucking *fellaghas*.

When they run into Fatiha, she's in the shade of a tree playing the olive game, but she stops right away when she sees Bernard. She runs up to him and asks if she can go see the turtle. Bernard says yes. So she gets her scooter that's against the wall of the house and comes back. Rabut asks her to stop for a minute. She's there, facing him, and behind you can see the house and its peeling façade.

He snaps the picture.

When she comes back to them, Rabut remains slightly behind them and looks at his cousin and the little girl, the two of them acting as if they were alone, there's no talking, it's very quiet, you just hear the voices of the other men further off, maybe a car engine. But that's all. On the sand you can see Rabut's shadow like a crawling animal, and when he looks into the viewfinder, Bernard is slightly leaning over the little girl, helping her by holding her up with one hand, she's very attentive to the way she's moving forward, very serious, almost grave.

Rabut wonders if she's wearing black because of the death of the doctor, he doesn't know that no one has ever seen her wearing light colors. In back, there is a building made of cinderblocks with a very low roof, and still further back, the hill and the sky of the end of the afternoon, almost ochre,

He presses the shutter.

And then soon all the platoons are in the yard, grouped under the flag. They walk back to the vehicles, already the engines are revving up, and in a few minutes the base looks the way it did before. Except there are tire marks and the dust raised by the trucks and jeeps seems to hang in the air, and all of them are thinking about the doctor, or rather, all of them are thinking that they've taken away his *remains*—that terrible word to talk about bodies, to talk about a man, like what *remains* of a skinned rabbit, of an animal skinned to be eaten, and they're all left with the weight of that absence, with the evening coming in, the dust falling slowly back down, so slowly you'd think it was floating, and then nothing, no sounds, just the men in the base and the routine to go back to, except that now everybody knows that what has been routine is no longer routine.

Because all of them already know that something has changed. They don't know what. Nothing's going to change. And yet, everything. They know mornings will have the same corporal's voice and the same old tune,

So-and-so! Java duty!

Transistors will be crackling out the first news of the day, voices will yell for them to turn it off, turn it down, and with eyes still half shut all of them will go take a leak against the little wall outside, a bit further off.

And yet, like all the others, without talking to anyone, Bernard immediately knows how it's not exactly the same as before that thing with the doctor; he knows the atmosphere will get bad and tense at the base, the others will no longer laugh at bedtime when there's only the little yellow lightbulb over them in the middle of the room, they won't laugh either when Février yells and keeps yelling,

Send us home, for chrissake!

Because each of them will think he heard his buddy's voice shake, something it didn't do before.

And the truth is that the guys can't find sleep, or that sleep comes very late in the night.

And when you hear how some men are tossing in their beds, turning, turning over again, you don't tell dirty jokes anymore, you don't talk about women; you only hear the silence and sometimes the exasperated, angry voice of this one or that one yelling for them to stop tossing around, cut it out,

Stop it for godsake!

And then the bodies will stiffen in the night, each man in his bed, and you know that for many of them it's almost impossible to breathe and hearts are near breaking, you can almost hear the urge to scream that's smothering them.

So under these conditions, more than ever you're overcome by nostalgia, by homesickness. And the days grow heavy even when the heat is not that stifling, even when you only have target practice. Because for the officers, too, something has changed.

They have a hard time keeping the men busy, making them believe what they do is important, useful, they know the men have lost their motivation; and now conversations are no longer so funny or lively, the days stretch out and the men seem to find sleep more at nap time than at night. You spend your time cleaning the barracks. Maybe you write even more than usual. You end up playing cards without even paying attention to the game. All you talk about is going home. They know that some of them will be eligible, others will have to settle for three or four days in Oran, and still others will have to wait.

They all pray, secretly, not to be one of those.

The ones who managed to get a week and will be leaving for France know that when they get back they'll have to report everything and tell a story that lives up to the expectations of those who have stayed behind. They don't know yet that they'll have to tell the story of a long, unpleasant trip, dismal barracks, hours of waiting for nothing, all that time lost, all that freedom wasted, the transit center and a night in the guardroom of the port, the night crossing, stretched out on the floor without seeing anything of the steel-gray water, and dreamless sleep.

They'll speak and the others will listen in total silence. They'll talk about the kisses and hugs, and that's it. They will say nothing more. The rest is for them. Friends, family, fiancée. And then sometimes no more fiancée, but news about her from other people, yes, she's with so-and-so's son. And they'll pretend not to hold it against her, and above all they won't try to see her again to demand an explanation, scream their disappointment and their feeling of injustice and abandonment.

They will know how to keep quiet, how not to tell the episode of the doctor, the villages. Perhaps talk only about the boredom and the routine. Better still: keep quiet and ignore.

A few days later, in Oran, it's someone you don't know who presses the shutter—and in the pictures there's a whole bunch of us, the tallest kneeling in front of the others, most wearing sunglasses, and most with a broad smile.

And then, among the pictures, there's the one Rabut will come upon in the middle of all the ones he took, without knowing how it got there. A shot he'll have seen at Bernard's place too, and he won't know who took it. It's Bernard with Idir, and both of them are laughing, squinting in the sun, you can see their teeth and prominent cheekbones, it's as if they were making faces at the sun, which is dazzling them. Bernard has put his arm on Idir's shoulder and behind them you see the war memorial, white as a cuttlebone and over it little French flags floating like a colony of insects, butterflies or bees, you can't tell in the blue air, it's July and the national holiday, carefully surrounded and watched over by the military. The parade, the French flags decorating the balconies.

It's a celebration, but it's also and above all a show of force.

But for them it will be something else: they're on leave.

And so you'll only think of the sun, you'll want to walk around, have fun, be your real age, something you occasionally have the impression of forgetting in the barracks or at the base. And so you'll have images, smells, and thoughts that will be etched into your memories as deeply as the knives of the fells into the flesh of their victims.

That will last all our lives, it will be as important as the rest and yet we won't realize how much it matters, because we don't think every day about the things that cover the walls of our lives; children with colorful paper cones full of chickpeas or salted pumpkin seeds, we'll remember them like we'll remember the

smells of sardines or merguez so intensely they become nauseating, nightmarish. But for the moment, it's the wind on the
waterfront and the light of Oran, the women with hennaed hair
and scarves tied around it, the little photographer's shops, the
rounded, worn-out cobblestones, the cars—Simca Aronde, Peu-
geot 203—the sun, of course, and the cicadas like static on the
radio, the trams, Philibert, Gisèle, Jacqueline, and Mireille's hand
when he touches her palm and fingers for the first time, at the
Mogador cinema in the afternoon, hesitantly at first, not daring
to look at her, but she turns frankly toward him and looks at him,
smiling, happy, not red and shy like he is but frank and simple,
as if the gesture had been the obvious thing to do from the start.

Like the others, he took a little room in a hotel near the station. A
cot that squeaks at the slightest movement, a sink with cold water,
a mirror cracked from top to bottom that splits his face in two
the way he splits the oranges he eats in the morning on his bed.

It's the first time he's had a room to himself in a long time
(he could say, since he was born); so what if the wallpaper has a
pattern of horrible flowers and the cockroaches have taken pos-
session of the sink and the mold makes the paper peel and draws
halos over the window and the sink. So what if the neighbors
fight for a good part of the night. He's alone in the room and
that's what counts, and from the window he can lean out and
look at the city, at the green and yellow trams.

And in the morning he walks around, he looks at the window
of the Grand Café Riche, at the Boulevard Charlemagne and the
little Rue de l'Hôtel de Ville. He pictures himself living here,
not even looking at the oval end of the building and the Café
Brésil anymore, which he knows so well by now. He tells himself
there'll be peace, he could live here and be happy. He likes the

atmosphere of the city. When he gets back to the base he'll write Solange and tell her everything you miss out on when you live in the country, like seeing all the young Arabs suddenly coming out of a back street in the afternoon with newspapers under their arms selling *L'Echo d'Oran*.

He has time to think, too, not just about the last events, about the corpse of the doctor and Châtel who's getting more and more sullen and doesn't speak to anyone anymore. He thinks about the Algerians; he tells himself that since he's been here the only one he knows is little Fatiha, and not even her parents, that the population is for him and the other men a kind of mystery that grows deeper from week to week, and he tells himself that without knowing why, he's afraid and doesn't know what he's afraid of.

He doesn't know anything, and as he walks through Oran very early in the morning, that thought makes him ashamed.

The more time passes, the more he repeats to himself and the more he can't help thinking that if he were Algerian he'd probably be a *fellagha*. He doesn't know why he has that idea and he wants to get rid of it very quickly, as soon as he thinks of the doctor's body in the dust. What kind of men can do that. The people who do that are not men. And yet. They are men. He tells himself sometimes that he'd be a *fellagha*. Because the peasants can't work their land. Because of the poverty here. Even if we're told we're here for them. We've come to bring them peace and civilization. Right. But he thinks of his mother and the cows in their fields, he thinks of the thick heavy clouds whose shadows fall on the animals' backs in the stream and on the poplars. He thinks of his father and mother, who had to put their hands over their babies' mouths—they told that story to him and his brothers and sisters many times—when the whole village left their farms to hide in the holes made by the shells and they could hear the steps of the Germans right near them. He thinks of what he was told about the Occupation, try as he might he can't help thinking of it, he can't help saying to himself that here we're like the Germans back home, we're no better than them.

He also thinks he could be a *harki* like Idir, because whatever you may say, France is not bad really, and then also because this is France too, here, it's been France for such a long time. And the army's a job like any other, Idir's right about that, being a *harki* means making a living for your family or else they'd die of hunger.

But he also thinks maybe all that isn't true. You can't believe anybody. They lie everywhere. He thinks he's been lied to forever. Something, lies. Everywhere. To the point of making him feel nauseous and overthrowing everything that makes up the world before him. He almost feels like crying. He doesn't know why. Why does he feel all blue and melancholy. When today. Four days. And Mireille as the sole horizon of these four days.

The sky is beautiful, so is the city, definitely, he has such a strong impression of the city, and the feeling that you can't live outside of a city. He's so dazzled by it that the speeches of the parish priest come back to him only as a new lie he hadn't suspected before, but now it's blatant: no, the city is not hell or temptation or superficiality, nor anything like that, and suddenly the priest seems ugly and bitter to him and for the first time Bernard won't open his missal for days.

He wonders if Châtel's way of thinking about God isn't closer to the truth than his. Then he stops wondering altogether.

Idir has asked him to come for tea at his parents' house. Bernard accepted, a little surprised at first. He doesn't have the impression that he's really close to Idir, but certainly more than he is to Abdelmalik, that's for sure, but that's pretty easy because it's also true that Abdelmalik doesn't talk a whole lot, not to him or to anyone. So, being close to Idir is the least you could expect.

When they greet him and offer him tea, Bernard is very impressed. And not just because he's in an Arab family, given the fact that he doesn't have a clue about the folklore and how they do things, but also because they go out of their way to entertain him, as if he were an important man, yes, that's what he feels and he's embarrassed a little because it's all too much, all the consideration, the friendship, the ceremony around the tea the mother is going to pour—and the grandfather who insists on showing him his veteran's medals, and his arm lost at Verdun that he talks about while he touches the emptiness in his jacket sleeve like a trophy, the sleeve folded back and stapled at the elbow; and the embarrassment, almost, which rises and suffocates Bernard as he faces Idir and his family, like suddenly the hint of a guilty conscience. He wonders why he should have a guilty conscience, about what, about whom, and he thinks again of Abdelmalik and what he had said to Idir,

We can do whatever we like, we'll never be French.

And he tells himself that this time he's dealing with things a peasant like him can't understand or can only have incorrect ideas about, he would have had to go to high school at least, gotten an education, experienced more things, met more people.

So he gets all flustered when the moment comes to say goodbye to Idir's family and thank them for their hospitality. He thanks them profusely, he stammers, he doesn't know why, he obscurely knows he won't tell anyone he's been here. And that thought bothers him. He wonders why he should be ashamed of coming here and yet he feels uncomfortable, as if he were betraying his own, but no, Idir is one of us, or maybe because he was especially embarrassed by the fact that they felt honored by his presence, he who made fun of *bicots* and *négros* back in the village, without ever having come across a single one except in the stories the grandfathers told about the Senegalese riflemen—giants they put in the front lines to scare the Krauts.

But ideas and questions evaporate the moment he meets the little group chaperoning Mireille. They give him a tour of the city, they explain the old prefecture on Place Kléber but the new one, no, you won't see it, it's hideous. Then the lions guarding the entrance to City Hall. And after that it'll be the Choupot neighborhood, and they'll stay in that neighborhood, with its ficus trees of the same green as the green benches where you wait for the trolley; and on the way back, Mireille points out the Météore on the right—we'll go there, that's where we go dancing, you'll see, it's fantastic, she says.

There's a record store. When Mireille points to one of the record jackets in the window, Bernard doesn't look at it and at first pretends he didn't hear. He wonders if he's the only boy his age who's never had records at home. Well no, he knows he's not the only one. He knows Mireille is pretty much alone in the opposite direction. He wonders why she can be interested in him, someone who doesn't know anything. He's willing to learn, but for that you'll have to admit you don't know anything, and this is something he absolutely won't do.

When she points to another record jacket, he doesn't answer, he walks ahead, he says anyway, for him, music . . . But Mireille then says she likes music enough for the two of them, she plays the piano a little but Chopin's really boring, but what can you do, it's my father. She'd rather play modern stuff, things you can dance to.

And speaking of dancing they'll go to Mirailles' across from the bakery, and at the bar they'll eat *kémias* and listen to the jukebox turned up to the max.

That's what they do. Mireille takes off her big green sunglasses that she leaves next to her like a little pet. The music covers up the conversations—Philibert invites Bernard to go snorkeling with him. He tells him he owns a little cabin out there on the beach; between Cape Falcon and Saint-Roch, when you leave the mountain there's a beach and the cabins are right up against the rocks, and Philibert says he spends lots of time there with his pals Lopez and Segura when they're not at work, and pointing to Mireille with a wink, he says to Bernard, it's a great spot to take a girl.

Later in the afternoon, Mireille has to go home. Guests are coming over, her parents insist that she get back early. Gisèle and Jacqueline are there to chaperone her, but they agree not to walk back with her and let Bernard take her to her door alone. He doesn't see the city, he would probably be unable to go back the way he came, and in fact he does get lost on the way back and if he hadn't bumped into Philibert, he might not have found his way back to the hotel.

It's because Mireille's voice is echoing in his head, like all promises made softly, calmly, as if you were just talking about the fine weather and cooing away to make yourself lovable and charming. But no, that's already done, they're already beyond that. With Mireille you talk about going to live in Paris, and even, without exactly saying it, getting married. Because even if the word is never said, you talk about the future and say: after the army. You say: what *we'll* do after the army, and not what he, Bernard, will do. But that *we* is dropped casually, in passing, and they both pretend not to notice it, as if the two of them were already married. And the parents don't matter. For him it's easy, he says he doesn't want to go back home.

He says: I'd like to open a garage.

That sentence dropping just like that. It's as if now he was suddenly so bold, as if with Mireille nothing was impossible. He will leave home, he will change his life, that's for sure, this time he knows it, there was a miracle and the miracle is her, right here, who came to him, he wonders what she can possibly see in him that's so . . . so . . . well, so, he doesn't get it, he can't see it, but okay, great, that's great.

He knows that sometimes the question becomes a source of worry, and the worry becomes pure anxiety. He's afraid that suddenly the miracle will stop just as it began, and he'll get a letter like so many buddies have already, a letter, a few words: *I don't love you anymore.*

He sleeps poorly, and the next morning he feels slightly nauseous. Février knocks on his door, they're going to spend the day together because tonight, already, they're going back. They have to be in the Oran barracks at five-thirty to be at the base early in the evening. They would rather have gone back the next morning, but that won't be possible. Nothing you can do about it, they know everybody has to converge on the barracks (and they all have to resign themselves, at least in spirit, almost despite themselves, whether they're in the city or further out on a beach, everyone already on his way in his mind, presenting himself at the barracks, telling the buddies two or three not so good jokes; and then, immediately, without thinking, making sure you're ready, joining the others, preparing the convoy, hitting the road and going back to the old routine).

The idea of going back to the base is terrible; Février and Bernard are struck with such fatigue that they don't even need to talk about it, because that's all they see, as each is a reflection of the other.

So: they'll talk only about the last three days.

Talk of what they'll have done. What it was like to find yourself for the first time without your buddies, alone at last, for once, a moment when you even felt somewhat abandoned at first, in a vacuum, instead of the pleasure you were expecting. And simply taking it easy, going to the movies, having a Pernod or a beer or an anisette and looking at the shop windows. Wasting time at the sidewalk cafés watching people on the street going about their business. And also, the buddies you ran into by chance and you spent the afternoon with them, and the evening, and then the next day too, and finally your whole time.

One part of the afternoon is spent at the Météore—the bar as you come in, the dance floor on the side. Everybody's breath has a little scent of anisette and couscous, and, for the women, the slightly heavy, flowery fragrance of lipstick and makeup.

Février and Bernard are excited, and at the same time tense; they watch the girls dance with other soldiers or men in civilian clothes, all in suits, with neatly combed hair.

They stand there for a moment without moving, they listen to songs, and despite themselves, they almost feel like dancing. Especially Février. And he doesn't hold back for long—why should he anyway, that's why we're here, to have fun, we've still got a few hours ahead of us and very soon he finds girls eager for a hand to invite them. They're sitting there looking around the room for a dance partner. Some of them are alone, and the idea that no one came with them goes to Février's head, and he doesn't wait for long to make up his mind.

Bernard is surprised not to see Mireille, nor even Gisèle, Jacqueline, or Philibert and his friends Lopez and Segura.

They'd made a date to meet here. And suddenly he gets worried. What if nobody came? If he had to go back to the barracks without having seen Mireille again? The idea seems unthinkable to him. So he stays like that, standing there. He hesitates to go back to the bar then says to himself the bar, yeah, why not, maybe, from there he'd see who comes in, rather than waiting here doing nothing and watching the others have fun. So he lights up a cigarette and, a bit reluctantly, looks around again one last time to see if he can't find the face of a friend in the crowd, aside from Février.

A friend, no. But a face he knows, yes, very quickly. Because as he walks over to the bar, among the soldiers he recognizes Rabut in the entrance, who hesitates for a moment then comes over and waves when he sees him.

I didn't recognize you, he says to Bernard.

And that's about it. They don't talk much. They stay next to each other, they tell each other that anyway they'll leave together for the barracks, yes, what time, five, if we want to be there at half past. They don't tell each other they could leave on their own, they don't like each other much and at the same time they stick together as soon as they see each other, that's the way it's always been, and it's even more true here, something from home that connects people without their really knowing why, through what old habit, so old they don't even think of questioning it.

Rabut orders a beer. He asks Bernard if he wants one and he shakes his head. He looks at the door, the people coming in, still nobody, none of the faces of the people he's waiting for.

And disappointment settles in.

The two cousins hesitate to go into the part of the club where people are dancing. Rabut glances in and Bernard doesn't say anything when he sees that look, he thinks maybe Rabut is waiting for Mireille, too.

Of course not.

He tells himself he's making up stories, it's not because Rabut and Mireille danced together once or twice that you necessarily have to imagine that they.

Then he wants to reassure himself by repeating that in love, trust is important, trust is everything, he has to trust Mireille, that's what Solange would explain to him, and Solange always gives good advice.

Trust her, yes.

Even if, of course, it's mostly Rabut he doesn't trust.

Finally, they go back to where people are dancing, they do it without talking to one another, just a nod, it's better than standing there glued to the bar. But Bernard looks at the entrance to the bar one last time and unfortunately no one's coming—that idea that nobody will come, he looks at his watch, will no one really come? He wonders if he'd have the time to go all the way to Mireille's house, it's not so far to walk, he thinks he could find the way again, even if he's not too sure.

He imagines himself ringing and knocking at the door. He imagines the face of the Arab woman opening up for him, letting him into the corridor; but perhaps they wouldn't open or from the entrance he'd be surprised to see a whole company of people at the dinner table in the living room or the dining room—or sitting in armchairs, uncles, aunts, all in fine, dark, strict suits and women in gowns in unfamiliar shapes and colors, and he'd be standing there under their half-amused, half-scornful eyes, with his cap in his hands and his thick smile, his thick face, the way he looks with his pleated pants, he tells himself that with his silly soldier's pride he'd just look ridiculous and grotesque.

So no, he won't move. They said the date was here. I'm not going to budge. If she ever arrived at the moment he was leaving for her house, it would really be too dumb. For him to get to her house and they'd tell him,

You must have passed her on the way, she left a good half hour ago with her friend Gisèle.

He's not going to budge. He's going to wait.

And so they don't talk, they just look at Février who's dancing and changing partners every time, trying his luck, sweet-talking into ears with earrings sparkling under the lights of the nightclub.

Then Bernard walks back to the bar and sits down. He has a beer and turns around as soon as people come in and he hears voices and women laughing. He remains alone for a moment, meets guys from his platoon who come in and go out very quickly saying see you later. He answers halfheartedly and suddenly surprises himself counting the bubbles in his beer as they rise and disappear, like the voices behind him. And then he tries to smoke again, he still has some cigarettes, a few, the soft pack in his pocket, and matches, then his hands shaking a little and suddenly he straightens up, is he going to wait like that? Is it possible to wait and tell yourself that you're going to stay alone at the bar when you've already been waiting for an hour and ten minutes, soon an hour and fifteen?

Rabut and Février join him at the bar, they joke around, laugh, they're talking loudly. Their laughter suddenly irritates Bernard, but he moves over so they can sit down at the bar with him.

They order two more beers.

Soon the pack of cigarettes is completely empty. Bernard crushes it slowly, very seriously, very, very slowly and carefully, until it turns into a compact ball, very tight, as concentrated perhaps as the ball of rage and anger he feels rising up inside him with great force—something of that furor he absolutely doesn't want today, a black knot forming now and he wonders what's happening, if he didn't make a mistake about where to meet, if he understood the time and place correctly, or something may have happened to Mireille and Gisèle, or to someone else, and then in that case why, why didn't any of the others come and warn him, tell him there's no point waiting for Mireille and hoping to see her today?

But nothing. No one comes. The music is unbearable. The perfume of the girls and the smell of beer. The men in suits, all of them dressed up, ugly, like everything is suddenly ugly, hurtful, loud colors, screaming music; and the air is suddenly as gray and full of smoke as his thoughts growing somber and dark, and he can feel the irritation and the perfume smelling too strong and making him dizzy.

He closes his eyes before ordering another beer; he tells himself he drank too much. He never drinks, or very little, and now his head is spinning. And yet he didn't drink much. But there's the sun, too, that heat he can't really get used to. The frustration. The tension. The fatigue from his bad night. That sudden fear, so strong, of telling himself that Mireille won't come back to him. That it's over. That she doesn't want to see him anymore. She's realized he's a simple peasant, a peasant's son, she realized that the other day, because of the shop window with the records and now she must think he's a moron and an ignoramus, she's laughing at him with the others, in another bar, and maybe she's even dancing with other men and his name is already like the name of a song that was a hit last summer and then,

Ciao, bello.

But no, that's stupid, it can't possibly be like that. He blames himself for always imagining things the same way, situations where he's always humiliated, brought down lower than the ground, as if he always had to end up that way, like a wimp, like a nothing, a less than nothing; and this time he doesn't want to. In fact, no, he never wanted to.

And he won't let them push him around.

He looks at the time. It's not time to go yet. But it's getting later, the clock is ticking, it's ticking so fast that soon he'll have to make up his mind and give up waiting here; he twists his neck around as soon as he hears new voices, bursts of laughter; he would recognize Mireille's laugh anywhere any time, so the idea of telling himself he'll have to leave before hearing her again, and seeing her—that idea seems almost terrifying all of a sudden, it's as if he felt himself losing his footing. Without being able to be more rational. Without knowing why, inside of him, the feeling is so oppressive, so disturbing.

And so he says yes without thinking, without knowing what they're saying to him.

Someone suggests another drink and he says yes without thinking or listening, even though now he has a stomachache and the smoke and the mix of odors are making him nauseous. And the other two with him insist on laughing and telling jokes, their voices so loud and their laughs so heavy, he hears that, picks up his glass and looks at the entrance one last time. He says he's going to leave. He's not staying here. The heavy laughs and the jokes Rabut and Février have told a thousand times are becoming unbearable, especially because he sees the jokes only as a way of provoking him, that's right, they're just taunting him, they've been teasing him for the last ten minutes at least, a sneaky way of looking for a fight, of annoying him still more, of laughing at him—and besides he thought he saw a gesture, for sure he saw it, Rabut nudging Février with his elbow.

He doesn't want to lose his temper.

He runs his fingers over his lips; they're dry, his mouth feels all furry. So, he swallows what's in his glass in two big gulps, very fast, and when he puts it back down with a sharp, brusque gesture, stronger than what he was expecting, the noise on the counter surprises him and he stares at Rabut and Février: in a curt, biting voice, not looking at Février but only at Rabut he throws out,

Hey, what's the matter, what does he want from me, the graduate's got a problem?

And a few hours later, some can say they saw Bernard and Février, and Rabut too, in a nightclub. Can say,

We saw them we said hi and we said see you later.

Very quickly, the word goes round in the barracks: some soldiers, draftees. Hey guys, some draftees are missing.

It's not quite what they think, not quite yet what the soldiers think but what they already fear when they contact the base back there—assassination, kidnapping, anything's possible, they know that, they don't trust this place, they pretend they're not thinking about it but they're always afraid something like that might happen, anytime and anyplace, so they reassure themselves by saying,

Nothing's for sure, maybe they only went to sober up someplace and that'll be it, they wouldn't be the first.

The two jeeps and the half-track are waiting under the sun in plain sight, in the yard. From the base, the corporal wanted to talk to one of his men: it was Nivelle. He ordered him to go look for Février and Bernard, and not come back without them.

Take Idir, he knows the city, and find those two assholes for me.

That's what he says before hanging up with a bang, very angry. And an hour later, Nivelle and Idir and two other men come back at the double, alone.

They say they didn't find anyone.

They say,

Yes, people saw them, some people saw them, a whole bunch of people saw them and when things went bad they disappeared and then nobody.

And in the barracks the men who know them are surprised and try to picture Rabut and Bernard under the sun, those two country boys, more country than ever, with Février around them doing his best to calm them down and failing, and they wonder how something between the two cousins exploded because Rabut must have drunk too much, too fast, that's what they'll be saying,

Rabut likes to raise his elbow in the rec hall but they know that the other guy, the cousin, no, he's kind of religious, a beer from time to time that's all, and he likes to play cards and maybe have a smoke with his buddies and kid around, but he's not the talkative type, quiet guy, a little gloomy, a worrier, and often his missal in his hands and prayers on his lips, that's what they know about him.

What they think they know, and nothing more.

You really wonder what could have happened and then very soon you don't even try to find out why, at the bar, Rabut suddenly looked at his cousin with that serious expression just because the guy had said something silly, not really mean. And yet Rabut had that cold, hard way of looking at him before answering, leaving his glass on the bar and straightening up just a little, giving him a kind of—how to say it, what can you call that—a shifty look and also that smirk, that determination not to pay attention to what the other guy had said,

What does he want from me, the graduate's got a problem?

Rabut not really flinching and holding himself back, and even ignoring (pretending to ignore) what he'd heard, as if he were just distracted by the bar, by the people too, and the music, nothing, a little mocking smile, not even a nasty look, for hardly a second and yet he couldn't let that go.

Hey, cousin! Drop it, don't start up with that again.

How then there was that ripple of motion, no one could tell how, how between them things went over the edge and the two bodies were carried away, first into the entrance, both of them, the two cousins, their bodies and shapes roughly the same size forming one single black and gray shape, with the shapes of their hands not yet clearly visible in the doorframe and the outside like a photograph or a painting or something too garish, the white light, blinding, and the ficus, the color green, motion too, and then just Février and voices around them talking, laughing, having fun with it, those voices getting much louder, not shouts yet between the two men, not their hands yet but already their red faces and their eyes open very wide like the eyes of corpses and owls in the night, they know all that by heart, but not yet what's coming, what they're going through now, what holds them and everything that was said at the entrance to the bar before someone decides they were becoming violent and they—so, to say how it all started, not just what led to the fight, but,

The *graduate*,

That word caught by Rabut, drunk enough that afternoon not to take it. That smile with that look. That smirk. How both of them rushed, not at each other, but to face each other, planted there, already set to fight,

Why do you have to fuck with me here, too?

Both of them tensed up in the doorway, not seeing anyone else coming in anymore or even hearing the voices and laughs at first, Février's voice, the voices of a few soldiers at the bar; and then a fist very tightly clenched, as tightly perhaps as a pack of cigarettes rolled into a ball and left there on the counter, and then, like a hand, a flower, opening on the bar, blossoming, going slack as it smooth's out slowly, like a small animal moving, a crab, sideways; and of course, at first no one thought they'd hit. You hear voices. Music. Life in the street.

And the doctor, when you found the doctor were you cleaning your nails so as not to look at him, did you call the doctor a slut too, when he died?

And Bernard, his mouth hanging open and the saliva shining, didn't answer right away; then his fists clenched,

You're a total asshole, Rabut, you always were an asshole.

Neither of them talking about Mireille while Mireille was the only thing on Bernard's mind.

He said to himself: Mireille.

Her name like a dream to hang onto. When his heart suddenly jumped, that's right, jumped in his chest and he straightened up because the other guy had straightened up and suddenly no peace is possible between them, no peace anymore because Rabut has pushed Bernard away and he has tears in his eyes when he whispers and spits in disgust—Bernard thought he heard it, he did, that name and that image, he's sure of it, from Rabut, the words in Rabut's mouth.

I felt like saying that to you for years, nobody ever had the guts to tell you,

Rabut with tears, no, eyes swollen, his voice shaky,

She was your sister and you called Reine a slut, that's what you were saying—slut,

And Bernard not listening, frowning, had started to spit,

What're you talking about, you don't know a thing, nothing at all, nobody knows anything, just shut the fuck up, Rabut.

And then the bodies and the shouts, not their shouts but the shouts of the others, all the others around them who didn't see or believe that it could start so fast, so hard, the sound of punches, the shock of punches to the jaw, the one who started punching the other, the bodies grabbing each other, fists clenched, necks tensed, chests thrust forward and the shouts, the threats, both of them out of breath, blindly pushing off everybody opposing them, interposing, and both of them together, united, in agreement on this at least, to clear space around them and struggle to get free so they could run at each other, straight ahead, spitting, the shouts are so loud and finally they're pushed outside, both of them thrown out and even kicked despite Février, despite other soldiers, with some people trying, with gestures, words,

Calm them down,

No,

Impossible with words they can't hear, gestures they can't see, hands they push away, impossible to do anything and certainly to calm them down, neither of them, together in it, impossible to shut them up.

Stop,

They saw nothing of the laughs or the bets already shouted out, and around them the mass of people and the hands imitating punches,

Go, go!

Hit him!

Hit him!

The hands like a hedge making a fence around them and the mouths of children full of watermelon, a few thin wisps of white clouds above them, the kids yelling and laughing and the women, worried, calling out to each other, looking for support, calling out under the oh's of stupefaction and the encouragements, some of them looking around and insisting, they have to be separated, who's going to separate them, nobody, their chests thrust forward, their hands clenched into fists, fake boxers, a cockfight, and others on the contrary yelling call the police, somebody, their voices drowned in the dust and under the blows, sharp, short, the fists, the breaths and then the shouts and the laughs.

And while they're hitting, neither of them can imagine or think of anything. And yet their hearts are emptying out, they don't know of what, either of them.

But they empty out.

And all around them the sun, the shouts and the people are like spots of color and remote, incomprehensible sounds, more remote than even the place where that need to hit is coming from. As if Bernard were hitting his mother. As if he could finally hit his mother as if she were a man and yell and howl out his hatred at last; like bursting a blister full of pus and vomiting out the image of the doctor's body—both of them have the impression that they're crying as they hit and by hitting the other it is themselves they are hurting.

And at that moment, Bernard cannot imagine that forty years later—let's say, almost forty, yes, almost forty years, so many years, all those years, he can't imagine that leap in time and, through the thickness of the years, see or even perceive that winter night when Rabut wakes up again with a start because in the course of the day someone will have said the name Algeria.

While he's fighting, Bernard doesn't imagine anything.

Not his voice, of course, nor the face he'll have forty years later. Not the day of Solange's birthday, nor the little deep blue jewel box he will have bought for her and certainly not Chefraoui nor the night that will follow, nor Rabut, fat, heavy, a little clumsy, waking up with a start at three in the morning as he does every time he has insomnia.

And this time like all the others, Rabut wakes up with his eyes wide open: that is, when he realizes he's awake, it's as if his eyes were already wide open, his hand groping in space trying to find the switch of the bed lamp. He's a little shaky, breathing hard. He wakes up in his bed next to his wife, Nicole, who has her back turned and hears nothing. He has the face and body of a man of sixty-two and he's tired, he feels so heavy, exhausted, there's drool on his mouth and he may wipe his fingers on it a few times to dry it, as he also does on his face as if to unwrinkle it, to retrieve his face from before, a smoother face so as to understand better, but no.

First he has to raise his body a little, and it's complicated, the pillow behind him slides down, flattens out, he has to turn a little to raise it and sit up but he's like a drowned man, he is a drowned man, he's drowning—and while he's trying to grab the switch of the bed lamp next to him, he still sees those images passing in front of his eyes, he still has to bear them and hear that old fight again, a fight that could have been stopped if only, instead of opening his big mouth—as he will blame himself so often for doing ever since—instead of opening his mouth and stirring up the man facing him who would pay so dearly for that fight, if he had only known, if he could have known, no, he wouldn't have stirred up Bernard's anger and then.

But then—

Bernard would be—he saved his life, too. Because of that fight, it's thanks to that fight that they didn't go back to the base that evening and were compelled to stay in the city barracks.

Yes. Except that if they'd gone back to the base nothing would have happened like,

   like,

like that.

And Rabut may well find himself sitting in his bed, worn, his body turned flabby from the years and the family, from all those weddings, births, communions, and the banquets with the North Africa Veterans, their *méchouis*, the nostalgia for something lost over there, maybe your youth, because maybe you end up embellishing even the memories you'd rather forget but can't get rid of, never completely. So you transform them, you tell each other stories, even if it's good to know you're not the only one who went there, and from time to time, have a laugh with the others, when at night you'll be all alone to face the ghosts and feel your hands sweat.

   And let yourself be taken over by the young man Rabut once was, punching away without stopping, without realizing he's taking punches too, how he's hurting and almost losing heart, when they start rolling on the ground under the shouting, and Bernard—Rabut doesn't remember that—Bernard grabbing his face with his fingers squeezing, scratching him, tackling him onto the ground, hitting him some more, faster and faster, hard, fists like a cleaver, a chisel, like stones, punches—but not the worst yet—he'll be in pain for weeks—still more pain for months—his head against the asphalt—the other hitting—fingers clinging, almost trying to rip his ears off—and the fists hitting the eyes—the body giving way—eyes closing—skin cracking—the other guy's on top of him—he's being crushed and soon feels only a huge fatigue and a great abandonment of his whole body—it's cracking, dislocating and the silence in his head, the blood in his mouth—a bloodbath in his mouth—the smell—his nose is bleeding, too—he's not breathing anymore and already words do not reach him.

And now Rabut can't really see the face of the man they take him to right after that, the man who saw the fight from his window and ran over with his doctor's bag and behind him his wife begging him not to get involved. But the man didn't listen to her.

He came there, sweating already, breathing heavily, in a short-sleeved shirt, with a handkerchief to wipe off his forehead, his face, and then words to separate the two men, to get help separating them. He wanted us to go to his house, even demanded that we come, that we be treated before we went back to the barracks or wherever you want to go, to hell if you like, but stop that and stop it right away, just stop it, he demanded. And now Rabut drags himself along, supported by him and Février, while Bernard lags a few meters back, walking reluctantly in their wake. Because yes, Bernard is there. He comes along without thinking, because ever since childhood he never has learned that he could let Rabut leave, go his own way; so he follows him without even thinking. Even if he doesn't help carry his cousin who's a lot more banged up than he is, all he can think of is following as he staggers along, puffing and panting with his head down, looking at the pavement and in the dust for a few minutes as if he'd lost his glasses or something, maybe his watch, and then giving up, resigned.

The doctor rolls up his sleeves and for nearly two hours lectures each of the two cousins alternately, seriously, diligently, calling Février to witness, who nods, yet glances at the clock he can see out there in the library. The doctor talks as he takes care of them, he talks and lectures them like a good father as he gives out compresses, with precise, supple gestures, so gently it's almost a caress, all the while repeating with consternation, as if we didn't have enough violence, guys, you shouldn't fight, you shouldn't get yourself all worked up like that, and so on, while behind him his wife silently serves them tea and cookies to cheer everybody up.

And during all this time Bernard says nothing. He answers yes or no, and that's it. He waits. He looks at the doctor from behind, at Rabut's legs and arms hanging over either side of the examining table. Bernard stays like that. From time to time he gets up, stands there for a few minutes without really knowing where to go, then walks over to them, comes back, sits down again. Then gets up again, this time very quickly. And he walks around, very straight, stiffly, then goes over to the window as if this time he knew why he was getting up, leans out and looks into the street, where they had their fight.

Everything else happens for them as if in a kind of fever. Like in a dream, or as if a part of that time—of their life anyway—had been erased. Their arrival at the Oran barracks means only prison doors shutting on the three of them, the time to sober up, despite Février's shouts of protest, the time, they are told, to think things over. And no matter how loud Février yells he has nothing to do with it, the only thing he can hear echoing through his head all night is,

You'll explain yourself tomorrow.

And what he sees: the door shutting on him, a tiny white rectangle where dilated pupils look at him for a long time, then disappear into the dark.

And the night. Three silences and shining eyes. Three solitudes. Nothing else.

Very early the next morning they're allowed to go join the others. Février doesn't talk to Bernard, because it's his fault he spent his night in the brig. He's cold, he's dirty, exhausted, and he didn't sleep; he knows he, too, will be tried along with the others for being late and for the fight too, and now that's driving him up the wall.

But all that was nothing, nothing at all, he'll later say to Rabut at the end of the sixties, when he came to tell him about Éliane and him, and the farm, and that he'd seen Mireille and Bernard with their first child: she was pregnant and sad, not old yet but about to fall into a state sadder and darker than old age, while he, Bernard, so different from the one who—

So no.

No, finding himself there in the convoy that was bringing us back to the base, so sad and angry, dirty too—that was nothing and I even have to try hard to remember that day, he would tell Rabut later, seven or eight years after all that, so amusing during the meal, talking about everything, very funny, really, and Nicole remembering him for a long time as a big oaf talking only about his own part of the country.

Whereas he also talks, especially when night has fallen and the wife and kids have gone to sleep, he talked that evening, talked so much even, about the events, years later, about their events, when they talked, finally, sitting there alone and already slightly drunk, about how they'd had such a hard time living since then, the sleepless nights, how they'd also given up believing that Algeria was war, because you fight a war against guys on the opposite side, except that for us, and also because in a war you're supposed to win, but there, and also because war's always bad guys against good guys and there weren't any good guys, just men, and also because the old folks used to say yeah well it wasn't Verdun, man did they ever break our balls with Verdun, that crap about Verdun, how long are they going to repeat that, and the others after that who saved our honor and all that crap but we, because as far as I'm concerned, Février had said, you see, I didn't even try to talk about it because when I got back nothing was there for me, work on the farm, animals to feed, and then watching the little car on the farm across from us that Éliane got out of every Sunday around five when she came back from her in-laws. Because when I got back, telling myself she was married, yeah, that was really rough. And to a neighbor, a loser I never had any respect for because I knew his whole family were collaborators in 1940, they changed sides at the last minute, all those bastards driving out the last Germans with shovels, that's what I was told, my father told me, nobody's more enraged than the Johnny-come-latelies, something to prove, to make up for, show they're on the right side, all that misery and all they cared about was being on the right side, to really be on the right side, I know, they told me about that twenty-year-old guy they finished off with their shovels and so to tell myself she married a guy from that family, because the son of a bitch got a medical exemption and had money, when I came back I didn't leave the farm for months, I even worked on it like never before, I fixed the fences, I walked through the country for hours and at the time I never thought mud was better than the stones back there, believe me, no, and the mud, the boots, the humidity, and the heaviness of the earth, how you sink into it, well, the only one I could talk to without screaming was my dog, when I'd walk in the woods for hours on end, and even at night he was the only one I could talk to.

Hey, it's still like that. There were guys like me in town. We never talked about Algeria. Except we all knew what we were thinking when we'd say yeah, we're just like the other guys, and animals are better than we are because they don't give a damn about the right side.

And when Février had said all that, it was also to speak about the silence of the next day when they left for the base, and how mad he was at Bernard for getting him mixed up in family quarrels, like it's so interesting, right.

And for years, Rabut was to repeat to himself, I don't know why I can't sleep at night anymore, I don't know if Algeria's the reason really, or if it's only because of Février coming here years later and telling me how it went when they got to the base out there, he and Bernard, and saw the big oil tanks like giants in armor to welcome them, and the wind. That morning there was wind, he said the wind was important because everybody's face was slapped by the sand and in your eyes the grains were burning, and on your cheeks the skin was red like it is from the alcohol you put on after shaving, he said.

And now, for years now, Rabut has been hearing Février's voice, and he can see him telling how the road was that morning, and Rabut, ever since, often wakes up as if he himself had seen that, as if he himself had been there but he hadn't, since he'd stayed at the barracks in Oran, it's just Février's voice that comes back to him.

And maybe also something of Février's terror and the terror of the other men.

All the others with him, in the jeeps, in the half-tracks, their bodies shaken by the road, the stones, the potholes, the road back, with the wind and the sand both hitting them at once and giving that taste of dust to the blue of the sky all the way down to the bottom of your throat; you can cough or drink all you like, nothing helps. Your hand in front of your mouth doesn't protect you, nor your closed lips, already dry from the start of the morning, even if it's early and the sun is not yet high in the sky, not completely blue yet but pale, hesitant. But there's nothing hesitant about the sand and the wind, which bother them like gnats in front of their eyes or lash at them like little lead pellets. And the almost light brown sky on the horizon and an endless expanse broken by—nothing, no, nothing breaks the horizon this time, nothing, not one of those vertical bars that should be telegraph poles, and no wires stretched between them either—because this time it isn't just one or two poles the guys have sawed down. They've done it on the whole length of the road. Some of the poles fell on the side of the ditches but others—maybe they did all they could, probably they did all they could to make them fall on that side—others fell onto the road, in a straight line from one side to the other, with the wires all tangled up and dragging through the sand like dead snakes, forcing the convoy to stop often, dozens of times, along the whole length of the road.

And then you realize it's like that as far the eye can see, soon you see that it's along the whole trail because further on there's a turn and the road goes down to the sea, so your eyes can take in the whole landscape far into the distance and from that far this time you understand that there's almost nothing else to see.

And that, Février had said, that got even me out of my bad mood and my anger at Bernard. As if suddenly you remember there are more important things—the things happening now, and the buddies, we look at each other, we exchange the same fear, the same questions, so what happened between us the day before or even two hours before doesn't exist anymore; we're welded together by the same fear, at that moment we share everything, the same looks. And the need to talk to each other, because now—with the convoy stopped at the side of the road, the guys speechless for a minute, then jumping out of the jeeps one after the other—it's as if the fells had done it calmly, without being afraid of anybody, that's what you feel at that moment, and all of us have the same thought: it's as if this time they're the masters here.

At first we tell ourselves it's like always and we'll leave it at that. Then we get going and very soon, all of us, we're there kicking at the ground to send the poles into the ditch; after that we get organized, one car drives ahead, stops at the first obstacle, three guys jump out running and pick up the pole, move it, and during that time the rest of the convoy moves forward, then stops and other guys do the same thing further on, while the first jeep passes them and so on. Like that the whole way, without talking. Except that as we go, we get increasingly irritated, and soon we're angry, all of us, not only because we're thirsty and already sweating and can't see the end of it. But we feel it's a provocation and we don't know how to respond, we're being trapped, we imagine the fells lying in ambush somewhere, laughing at us, we imagine them—we always imagine them since we can never see them, and anger can't do anything, just give us the additional energy to get it over with faster and clear off the road very quickly while keeping inside ourselves the urge to scream at this whole country, at the stony trails, the brush, and the olive trees, at the wind, and the sea, at everything, the sky, the brambles, the tufts of grass, as if everything were looking at us and laughing along with the fells,

Come on, come out and fight if you're men, show yourselves if you're men—rather than this solitude, this dejection setting in already, and that discouragement coming over you when you hear the brakes of the jeep stopping a dozen meters further on.

Then the jeeps finally crawled into the base, and now we're all extremely irritated. We don't talk, we just look around, quick glances that don't really focus on anything, on anything in particular, quick glances, that's all, to fill up that huge silence, that space too huge as well, yet so familiar, but we look at it as if for the first time, as if it were a cave, a forest, with fear in our guts, our rifles at the ready, our hands sweaty and shaking. We don't look for long, though, because very soon the quick glances are for each other.

And it's not to look for an answer to something we don't understand, it's to give ourselves the strength, the courage to go forward, not to understand.

Because that, no, no, we can't understand that, there's nothing to understand.

Why suddenly we are so afraid of that silence and still more of what it might mean. We're scared and suddenly it's not for us that we're scared, not for us, but for them, inside, inside the base—and those engines idling, even the road seems flatter than usual because when you drive less quickly you don't feel the potholes so much and that reassures no one, just as none of us are reassured by the silence. And not one of us says anything. We can't. Silence. We wait. We're driving very slowly and we can hear the gravel and the pebbles crunching under the tires. Our hands on our rifles, our hands too cumbersome almost, that sudden tingling in our hands all the way down to the tips of our fingers. And then the hills. The brush. A few trees by the side of the road and the sea down below and the big oil tanks, still untouched by the sun that hasn't yet sent its blinding flashes off the oil tanks like it sometimes does in the afternoon.

The moment of getting to the base and already discovering that weird picture: who says it first, who dares to say it, give it a name and say,

Jesus, did you see—no, I don't know who says it.

Only, something travels very fast from one pair of eyes to another. And you try to understand. Or rather, try not to be overwhelmed by what you're thinking, by what your eyes have seen. So you say to yourself, where's the sarge, someone has to decide what to do because all of a sudden we don't know what we should do, or think, we stay there and suddenly the vehicles instead of moving forward and starting the drive downhill after the last turn, slow down and brake. You hear the emergency brakes, the grinding of the axles, and the whole convoy comes to a halt.

And we wait.

We see this from above, from the road: in the yard of the base the flag has not been raised. The mast stands there, empty, the flag is not flying. Nobody says it yet, they just point it out to the others with a move of the chin.

Then someone says it.

The flag's not up, they didn't raise the flag.

We don't know what to think. Or do we already know? Maybe we do. Yes, already. We know. Do we know? It's only later that we tell ourselves we already knew, at that moment, and we just didn't dare say it to ourselves,

Yes, that's it.

We stay there for a few minutes, and a few minutes seem like a very long time, with the engines idling and rattling the metal of the vehicles, and us inside, until we hear the voice and the names, five names dropped from the voice in the first jeep, and it's those men who have to open the march and jump out of the jeeps, on the ready.

And of course the first names are ours. Bernard's and mine. We're the first names, followed by three others.

But us two first, because. Because. Soon they'll be saying all of this happened because we weren't there when the time came to leave the Oran barracks, and in a way we'd done the fells' work for them.

Yes, some said that.

Like we needed to hear that. As if the two of us, Bernard and me, hadn't already thought of that; if the convoy had left on time, then yes, it was hard to imagine what would have happened and to tell ourselves, yes, because of us. Maybe because of us. And how many times did I tell myself, I should have shaken Bernard and his cousin harder and dragged both of them, well, just Bernard, because after all, what did I care if Rabut got back to his barracks or not, what did I care when for me the only one who mattered there was Bernard, and I could never tell myself it's because of that fight and because we got there too late, they waited for us, it was the lieutenant's orders, his or the corporal's, or some sergeant, or somebody at the base, and really we couldn't do anything about it, they're the ones who made the decision to stay, and not leave without us, to wait for us, to delay the convoy's departure, it's not we who decided that everybody had to wait just because two guys weren't there on time.

Not sure it would've changed anything. Not certain. As if that would have changed anything. I didn't tell Bernard at that moment and he didn't tell me either, but of course we knew it would have changed things if the convoy had left, instead of waiting for us, the fells attacked because they learned we weren't leaving—they were informed, almost half a garrison less, that means something, they knew it, otherwise they never would have dared and that's a fact.

And nobody needed to tell us that it was because of us.

No.

They didn't need to say,

It's your fuckup, your fuckup—and so they all were careful not to talk to us, to turn away from us, to lower their eyes before us, change the subject, walk past us, look down on us. How I had to live through that with Bernard, too. Thinking back to certain images was maybe the worst: our beds untouched, neat and clean. The brown blanket carefully folded over the bed. And the snapshots near the pillow, tacked to the wall, smiling at us. For me it was Éliane's picture and for Bernard the postcard of the glowing Blessed Virgin with her hands folded and her tearful ecstatic look, while all around there was that silence and carnage with only that goddamn turtle raising its black wrinkled head, swaying a little, its little black eyes blinking, shining like a cat's eyes at night or the chrome on a car, the innocence of a little old lady crossing a minefield without anything ever blowing up in her face.

So afterward you can always say that it was Bernard's fault, my fault, Rabut's fault, whoever you want to blame.

It's mainly the fault of the ones who did it.

And then, Février had said, I don't know how you could describe the fear, when you're moving forward in silence with your body at an angle, your legs bent, your rifle in your hands, almost squatting—I mean, at the moment we were opening the road to the base, the few meters like that, all five of us, me in front, followed by Bernard, and the three other guys behind us—so scared that for awhile you end up not thinking about your fear at all, or about anything. You don't even know why you're moving forward. So you cling to your weapon and you run. You run head down, you advance in that silly posture, like a crab or whatever, to make yourself small and unobtrusive. And the hardest is not to scream.

You'd like to scream and you know you should think about all the hours you spent learning what you have to do, how you have to do it, things a soldier has to know, as if now we were in a war, and yes, we are in a war and we are soldiers. Men, like our parents and grandfathers, especially the grandfathers, dreamed we'd be, and later we will wonder,

Were they scared shitless like that at Verdun or in 1940? Is it the same fear in every war?

And really, I don't know anybody, absolutely nobody, who could fucking tell me that. And I say yes, it was a war, a form of war. We don't know what war is, but it sure does feel like war. I just know your breath is so loud you have the feeling the whole countryside can hear us breathe.

And I do remember how it feels, the pressure of the wire fence under my fingers, and the gate as if already opened, nobody's there, no patrol, no one, not one of our buddies. We look at each other. We hesitate to call out. Bernard signals better not to. Then we had to give it a little push with our hands, just a little, no need to make a big effort. A sharp push and the gate swings open.

It's not locked. It should've been. It should have been, of course it should have been locked, but it wasn't and so when it opens you should hear it creak but all I can hear is my breathing, so hard my chest could burst, and the sudden weight of the clothes on my skin and my neck so stiff it's hard to turn around and look at Bernard. Who is looking at me. We don't understand. We don't want to understand. What we can tell ourselves at that moment, the gate opening and not resisting as it should, the mast standing straight like that, with no flag, nothing, and nobody, still nobody, we tell ourselves it's impossible, the word is rolling in our mouths,

It's impossible, impossible,

And the word crumbles and falls away and is nothing but that soft paste dying in your throat, because fear, anger, fear again, so much fear, and you don't think it's real what you're going through, what's happening, and the idea you're making it up, forming in your mind, is so ridiculous, when we look at each other a few times to say,

Come on, move, I'll cover you,

And that ridiculous idea of covering each other too, of telling each other seriously that they simply forgot to wake up in there.

When we know how outrageous it is to think that.

But it's also a way of not screaming, of not screaming out the names of our buddies, we'd like to see them appear suddenly, right there. But, no. Silence. So we cover each other as best we can. We say let's cover each other because behind you, in your back, there is somebody shaking, ready to fire all around if anyone kills you. If anyone fires. If anyone moves. We cover each other. It's something to do. Like run and let an idea go by in your head, then another, then none, nothing, and signal behind you to move forward.

Then another guy comes. Bernard is right behind me. Then another. There are three of us. Then four. Then five. And then all the others, watching and waiting. And then the steel door, the one to access the lookout tower; we find it open, when it's supposed to protect the guy up there in the sentry box. It shouldn't be open either, we know that but we don't say anything. We don't say yet that they needed a key, we just say we have to go up there.

And we do.

With three of us staying down below and the other two taking the stairs. And then, right away, as we go up, we know we'd like to walk more slowly, we're ready to fire, we know we can fire but our fingers are hard now, stiff, and yet they're trembling, everything's trembling except the concrete steps under our feet and Poiret up there, his body tipped backward bathed in his own blood and his eyes wide open looking at nowhere.

The questions didn't come right away but very soon, Février had said, yes, very soon, because we find the door to the tower open too, not broken or anything, not a scratch, just open. They must have had a key. That's what we tell ourselves—but before that, Février had continued, there's this disgust and how I ran back down and almost fell, my scream running down the steps, shoving Bernard on the way down, Bernard's the one who told me, my scream, and also how I threw up but I think I don't remember that at all, and yet I can still see myself standing there, with my legs shaking and my anger even, a terrible feeling of revolt; it was a huge, I don't know what kind of fury it is when you see all your buddies one after the other with their throats slashed open, as if they didn't have the time to get out of bed, I don't know, you can say what you like, what you can, you can try to tell it, to describe it, you can imagine, try to imagine but in fact you can't imagine the silence you discover when you enter the room, that silence is so heavy it weighs down on your ribcage and it's as if you were at high altitude, like feeling the air pressure, and you're suffocating, first because the light's on in the middle of the room, that one bulb with its yellow light vibrating and you know that vibration well, you've been complaining along with the other guys from the start, you've been complaining about it with them and about everything, and some of your friends are here, they're dead and you see that, you see it, how they struggled, you know that, they're here, some of them are dressed, they had the time to get dressed, some of them, and to fight, not all of them, some are in their beds and the blanket's even on them as if they didn't see

195

anything coming. But others, no. And on those guys, there are marks of blows, they smashed their heads in with rifle butts, that's how Châtel died, from rifle butts, the front of his skull smashed in, and the time it took to slaughter them, all of them, the Kabyle smile, the thickness of the skin and the strange expression it gives to the face, like a mask put over the head, but the head is nothing, nothing, another mask and underneath there's nothing, the thickness of the skin, the blood, opaque and brown, and the stench heavy and rancid already, revolting, we don't stay long, it's impossible to stay there and see that, guys you know, all of them, and also the place, the room, and also how they took the weapons from the little armory where they were stored.

We don't think of Abdelmalik, not yet, but very soon we will, and it's not as if we just had doubts about him, but this proof, his absence, he disappeared, he ran away, and somebody opened the gates—who besides him—someone killed the two guys on duty in the night—who besides him—the night patrol, and killed them from the inside, no one knows how he managed to kill both of them, all alone, how he did it, or maybe he killed Poiret first, up there in the tower, then opened the gate and they came in one after the other, and he had the keys. And to think how Abdelmalik could have done it, and watch the others do it, killing just like that the guys he'd lived with for months, telling yourself, is that possible, not to betray or change sides, but to slaughter guys you joked around with and you knew that for them, the war, the independence and the liberation of a country—they were more or less okay with it, but basically what they wanted mostly and above all was just to get it over with and go home.

How he could do that, I'll never understand how it's possible.

And how is it possible to do what we discovered later, me and Bernard, the two of us, again the two of us, when we had to open

up the house and discover Fatiha's body and Fatiha's parents and
the little baby, all dead, dead, so, how

how people can do that.

Because, it's, to do what they did, I don't think you can say
it, I don't think you can even imagine saying it, it's so far from
anything, to do that, and yet they did that, men, men did that,
without pity, without anything human, men took an ax to kill,
they mutilated the father, the arms, they ripped off his arms, and
they opened the mother's belly and—

No.

You can't.

And I can't get that out of my head and it's no use gulping down
all those pills the doctors give me, Février had said, I can take thousands of pills, and work my ass off on the farm for days on end and
even think every evening about facing the night again, no, I keep
turning it over and over in my head and I still can't understand.

And I can't understand either how they could try us later,
Bernard and me. And how we had to hear not that maybe our
being late had saved the life of everybody in the convoy and ours
too, but how it was because of us that the fells had been able to
operate. And out of all of us, Idir's the one they got after the most,
so he'd tell what he knew. He was suspected of knowing, and he
said sometimes he suspected that Abdelmalik might betray us but
he didn't think he'd do it. He didn't think so and yet Abdelmalik
betrayed all of us, and he betrayed Idir as well, because twenty-
three thousand francs a month, that's not enough after awhile,
it wasn't enough to justify what he thought was treason to his
people, and Idir, who had almost seen it coming, had refused,
just as he refused, he said, to believe Abdelmalik was speaking
seriously when he started saying that anyway whatever he did,

he or someone else, they'd never accept him as a real Frenchman, that a real Frenchman couldn't be a man like him, like them, not a dirty Arab, since basically Abdelmalik ended up thinking all of us were racists and it would never change; he ended up turning against us but Idir didn't want to believe it, he didn't want to believe what he could actually see, every day on the base, getting more and more true, because when they asked him if he, Idir, had doubts too, about himself, did he understand that, he hesitated before answering: he said that he was French and as long as he was French he had no reason to betray his own flag.

And afterward, for months, when you're back home, Février had said, you find it bizarre that nobody asks you anything.

And me, like everybody else I read the paper and I saw in the paper that it was all over, Algeria wasn't French anymore, the war was lost, but nobody in the café ever mentioned it. There are the old folks playing cards. There's the warmth and the question of whether there'll be enough animal feed this summer.

When I go to the café, people who haven't seen me for a long time look at me and tell me I got thinner and I look like a man now.

Yeah, that's right, I am a man.

They ask what Algeria was like, and sometimes, the ones who are interested say it's a shame, all that for nothing. But still they're glad it's over and then. And then they go on to something else.

How are your parents and two more arms to take in the hay, that'll be good for them.

And at that moment I would really like to see the faces of those old folks in the café, the old men over their cards and all the others behind the bar, if instead of answering with a smile and with yes, if I told them what we saw, what we did, how long it would be before the owner said,

Shut up, that's enough.

How much would I have to tell them about the guys we let go and then shot in the head and kicked into the ravines to be eaten by the jackals and the dogs?

And finally, you tell yourself it's as if you never left. As if Algeria never existed. I remember going through a few weeks like that, when I began to eat well again and work and even make plans, turn the page, everything's the way it was before, Février had said, because old lady Fontenelle looked out from behind her curtain, because the hens kept pecking around on the path without paying attention to us, because of the smell of cow dung, the puddles of water, the plastic boots, the mud in the same old spots, and you hear yourself thinking that you'll have to lay down some cement in front of the entrance to the goddamn barn one of these days, as if you'd never left.

And mostly, I did all I could not to think.

But the truth is, the main thing on my mind was Éliane and I did everything I could to avoid her.

And in the evenings—I mean, at night—when sleep fell on me, inevitably I lowered my guard, and then it would come back, I would tell myself,

Thursday, next Thursday I'll go to the market,

Where I knew she sold eggs and vegetables, but not to tell her how she had hurt me.

I would wake up and that urge would be burning in me, the urge to plunk myself down in front of her and say,

What the hell do you think we did over there, what d'you think, tell me, while you were running away with, while you, with the other guy, you don't know, I, meanwhile I saw guys of twenty or twenty-five and even once I think he must have been seventeen but a *fellagha,* whatever his age was, I remember his screams and how he was struggling when we put him on the helicopter and the racket the blades were making over the sea and he was screaming, he was begging, and I saw the terror in his eyes—you know what that's like, do you? Did you already see that at your market, did you see terror in someone's eyes? You have no idea, Éliane, you have no idea about anything, we put his feet in a block of cement and let it take, and when the cement was hard we brought him into the helicopter and I swear he would've sold out the whole world, he would have informed on the whole world and if you were in his shoes you would've informed on the whole world too, except he had courage, he'd resisted being beaten with a cane, you should have seen his back, so black, so black—

While she—if I'd told her that—she would've drawn herself up scandalized, she would have said to me,

But it's over between us, it's over, I'm married, get the hell out of here, leave me alone, you're driving away customers with your stories,

And at the market the old women would have looked at me thinking who's that nut,

What's that nut talking about?

And Éliane would have looked everywhere, frightened, ashamed, for her husband, a relative, someone to come save her and free her from me, but I'd keep going,

If anyone resisted we threw him naked into the wash water of the trough, in the courtyard, and his body under the sun, and still more beatings with a cane, you don't want to hear that, she'd lower her eyes and say,

Shut up, shut up, stop it, shut up,

And the old women would say,

That's enough,

And the old guys would say,

That's enough,

And then I would say he had stood up under all of that, but when we plunged his legs into the cement he realized right away and he would have given everybody's name so as not to hear the blades of the helicopter and he did betray everybody—the cave where he and the others had been hiding, the materiel, the network, the recruiters, the escorts, the accomplices—and his hands and fingers hanging on so hard we had to cut them bloody and then hit, hit, and even then it seemed he couldn't let go; but his body did let go and his scream disappeared into the blue air of the Mediterranean under the noise of the blades and the indifference of the sea.

And the afternoon hours, smoking while I watched the cows and the river, listening to the poplars rustling in the wind, waiting for what.

How many times did I nearly get up at night and go wake my parents, force them to listen to me, imagine them sitting up in their bed with a start, all frightened to see me suddenly appear in their room at any hour of the night.

And smile to them, lean over toward their deaf ears, and them half frightened to see me so close to them, in my pajamas, my eyes shining as if from fever, as if I were drunk, with the ticking of the clock to accompany me and them not quite out of their old peoples' sleep, still half snoring, their eyes swollen with sleep, their bodies still slow and their blood so cold in their veins it prevents them from reacting, I imagined them, how many times did I nearly jump from my bed in the middle of the night to run into their room at the other end of the hall and storm in with gunfire in my voice to say that I had seen—me, their son—I had seen guys from here, local boys, white boys, do some funny things, and not just the wackos who'd fought in Indochina, while you thought I was preserving peace, well, me and my buddies on weekends we'd go out into the desert in jeeps and had races and sometimes, often, we'd hunt gazelles, and I would picture my parents' faces when they heard me say we rode after gazelles in the desert and we'd yell, bare-chested, standing in the vehicles, and my urge to force them to hear, to listen to the very end, to this, the gazelles running up into the hills to escape, and running into the sun to blind us—we could see their silhouettes, the little clouds of dust and their tawny white coats, and their sharp horns and then.

And then. Then nothing.

Nothing.

I remember all of it, Février had said.

That was on the evening he'd come to Rabut's place to spit it all out, because, even if he laughed while he said it, even if he told things in an almost casual tone, he'd finally confessed that his desire to see his buddies again was mostly his need to say everything that had been festering inside him and was becoming unbearable, too present, and he'd told himself that by talking with people like him he could, as he had said, root it out of himself.

But no.

He'd seen them all, one after the other.

The truth is that you don't talk about the past, you have to keep going, start over, move forward, not stir things up. But Février had remained alone, hearing them repeat, again and again, like an incantation or a prayer, this little phrase,

Start over.

And in the end, no one had wanted to let him talk. So he went to Rabut's, the one he knew the least, but the last one he'd been in close contact with.

For years Rabut's been sleeping badly, he looks for answers and trembles when he imagines he's found some.

With his buddies from the North Africa vets group they get together on Saturdays for banquets and they have fun. They think about their buddies, about the Algerians too, how it could all have happened, how sorry they are about all that.

That's what he tells himself.

And tonight again he'll wake up and remember and wonder if it's because of the cold that he's shaking, that his body is shaking, or if it's because there's this voice inside him that can't keep quiet and whispers memories as if in a minefield or a field of ruins, words, questions, images — a compact, vague mass and all he can get out of it is fear and a stomachache.

He's going to get up and take a pill because he'll say he has heartburn. Or his throat's too dry. Maybe a headache. And maybe make himself a glass of warm milk, with honey, to relax.

No.

Because the images from those old days keep coming in despite himself. And Rabut gets up as he has on so many nights, around three, sometimes four. And then he'll remember Février telling him,

We were caught in a sort of funnel, spiraling downward so fast, so violently, that's when we stopped calling them fells, that's when we started saying fucking Arabs or sand niggers all the time, because by that time, as far as we were concerned, we had decided they weren't men.

And like every time he'll have to say to himself,

Wake up, Rabut, get up.

He'll tell himself, better get up and be totally awake instead of lying in bed in this state, half asleep.

And that night, thinking about Bernard and Chefraoui, about Solange, and the stupidity of the past day, of that day.

Will I go over there tomorrow, to Bernard's place, with the gendarmes?

Will I have the strength?

Will I—

I got up and took my bathrobe, Nicole was sleeping, I was careful not to wake her—but she's used to hearing me shuffle along to the bathroom to relieve myself before sitting down in the kitchen and waiting for the hours to go by, over a cup of herb tea or something, anything to fill up the time—and that night, well, that was like the worst times, when even if I wake up and get out of bed, neither the anxiety nor the images go away.

And days like today. Bernard's face and Chefraoui's frightened look.

And then it all comes back.

And me, like a jerk, at sixty-two I got scared of the dark like a little kid, I had to turn on the light, straighten up, get up and walk out of the bedroom, splash some water on my face to refresh myself, yes, and refresh my memory, too, whereas all you want is for your memory to leave you the hell alone, finally, and let you sleep.

I thought about all that again, and I was saying to myself,

What has escaped me? What is it I didn't understand? Something must have gone right by me, something I saw or lived through, I don't know, something I didn't understand.

That's why instead of going into the kitchen and sitting down to stare into space or wait for the milk or the water to finally heat up in the little saucepan, I walked over to the front door, because there's a closet in the hall.

There's a whole bunch of things in there, odds and ends, that's where we put cans and bottles of water and milk. But you have to climb a little, that's what I did, I put my foot on the edge of the bottom shelf, grabbed the upper shelf and that way I could hoist myself up, stay standing and see all the way up, what was there in front of me, a pile of more or less useless stuff, all the way up, board games and checkers, old mismatched buttons in a plastic box, and at the back that shoebox and with it, still further behind it, almost inaccessible, the old Kodak in its case.

I grabbed the shoebox and walked to the living room. I put the box on the coffee table and turned on the lamp. I stayed like that for a while, hesitating before opening the box.

There's no need for a bright light. The little lamp and its emerald green halo, too weak to light up the whole room, is enough.

Why am I doing this, what am I looking for?

And I also wondered how many years it had been since I looked at these old snapshots, years so far back I had trouble counting them.

And I was saying to myself,

Rabut, you're sitting here over a shoebox, and you're going to take those pictures out, why will you do that? To look for what? There's nothing inside, no answer, I know every one of those pictures, I already know what I'm going to find.

I opened the box anyway, and in the Kraft envelopes I could feel the thickness of the stack of pictures, a particular set in each envelope, a format, dates written in pencil or ink on the back and sometimes names of towns that meant almost nothing to me anymore. I told myself that soon the dates and towns wouldn't mean anything to anyone, nobody would know the stories behind those pictures or even what the names and places on the back meant.

And I had to smile: I was so naïve I even kept trolley tickets.

I opened the envelopes and all the photos fell onto the coffee table like playing cards, and for a second I couldn't tell which ones I wanted to see or what I expected from them—because I'd given up trying to understand the words I'd heard from Février a long time ago.

I picked up the first pictures I had in front of me.

I leaned over the photos and looked at them one after the other. Slowly at first. Then faster and faster. Pausing over some of them and on the contrary passing quickly over the others, sometimes coming back to them, because of a detail, a question, a face. And of course I recognized people and places, streets, public squares, barracks, the base where I'd taken Bernard's picture and little Fatiha on her scooter.

I looked a long time at the photo where she's facing the camera and behind her you see the façade of her house. I looked at her face for a long time, her serious, almost grave look. And then, too, the fact that she's dressed in black.

I remembered why for years I hadn't been able to look at that face, its toughness, and also what I'd already told myself at the time: right away, very quickly, it had become almost, how can I put it—unbearable. Because all of a sudden her eyes were like an accusation. As if she were holding us responsible for her death, for everything, for the war. As if the fact she was dressed in those dark colors meant she was already dressed in mourning for the slaughter to come, as if she were in mourning for herself, in mourning for her own death.

I remember. Like a promise of suffering, whereas you'd like to see, in childhood, a promise of—it's a dumb word, really—of happiness.

I also remember when Bernard had written me.

He'd been sent out there to the far end of the Aurès Mountains or into Greater Kabylia, that, too, I don't know anymore, not too far from the desert, and I had spent a little time in jail because of that fight and I got that letter from him—I could have looked for it, it must have been there, somewhere, in an envelope. I didn't look for it. I didn't want to look for it. I hesitated, but then, no, what for? Why read the same words and see that blue ink from his Bic on a page from a school notebook again, where he was asking me to send him the pictures I'd taken of Fatiha?

I can still see myself reading that letter the first time, and how stupefied I was to find only that request about the pictures and nothing, not a word about himself, about that damned fight, nor about afterward, everything that happened afterward and that day after which we hadn't spoken to each other again. The coldness, the detachment of his letter. As if we hardly knew each other. Just asking me for the pictures, and without saying anything about anything, his new posting, how he was, how I might be after all that, and say, I don't know, something about what had happened.

No. Nothing. Just a polite request and his address.

I remember standing there stupefied because of the way he was acting; and that anger at him rising inside me. Then, after a few days of hesitation (because at first I was even determined not to send him the pictures at all, I'd written that to Nicole, not to ask her opinion but only to tell her mine, and then I had some doubts), I ended up giving in, finally I gave in and I can still see myself preparing the snapshots, sealing the envelope, I remember sending him copies of the prints, I'd just written a little note on a card hoping he got them, nothing more. I would have liked that indifference to be natural in me, too. But no. I had to force myself. Because I could have talked to him about everything, and at that moment I even would have felt like it. I could have told him about how afterward I hesitated to apologize to him, because I had said Reine's name and I shouldn't have. Because in fact the silence between us was precious, and should have been left unbroken.

I could also have told him about the tribunal.

We'd seen each other there once, very briefly, we just glanced at each other without saying anything, like ghosts, strangers passing each other, thinking they've seen that face somewhere before, when we were tried for our lateness, to determine how much was due to negligence, if complicity was involved, and so on.

He and Février wanting to be punished. They'd asked to be punished and came up with nothing better than to be sent off where they could really fight.

And the army was only too glad to comply: volunteers were rare.

I looked at the photos with their scalloped edges, and I ran the fleshy part of my fingers along the white frames that are slightly raised to emphasize the border of the picture, and at that moment I thought that in Algeria I had put the camera in front of my eyes only to prevent myself from seeing, or only to tell myself I was doing something—let's say, useful. Maybe.

Afterward, I never took pictures again.

I stayed like that and didn't really see the minutes passing, and soon more than an hour had gone by without my noticing it, because I'd been sitting there in front of the photos. And contrary to what I had thought when I told myself what's the point of looking at them, what for, I know them all, I know that none of them will give me any answers, I know there is no answer, but. What if.

They said things.

They say things. What things. Behind the faces, first. Yes, you can see them well, those faces of young guys of twenty. All those guys I knew, today their names are fading away faster and faster and I mix them up, I take one for another.

The dates, behind the pictures, like codes that have become useless, all those dates diligently written with a pen, in a fine, elegant hand, as if I weren't the one who'd written them but someone else, Nicole maybe when I got back, she's the one who wanted to sort them, name them, I don't know. Only, there were young men in the pictures and me, at three in the morning, I saw them smiling at me and joking, too, playing cards, posing bare-chested in their shorts, their sunglasses, I remember what we used to wear, actually I remember everything pretty well, us, what we used to say. And yet it's something else, it's smiles, kids playing, they're there in front of me, and I find them so skinny, so delicate and carefree, and the friendship between them, too, they're posing with their arms around each other's necks, they're laughing, clowning around, you'd think it was the schoolyard at recess.

The fear in your belly. But where is that fear? Not in the photos. None of them show that.

So what is it, what is it that remains, exactly?

I was saying to myself, I'm sixty-two years old and here in this living room, at almost four in the morning, I'm looking at photos and my eyes, the tears, the lump in my throat, I'm holding on so I won't collapse, as if the smiles and the youth of the guys in the pictures were like stabs of a knife, who knows who we were, what we did, you don't know, I don't know anymore. No matter how much I look at the pictures and see us again, the guys, photographed in Oran in nightclubs, at the Météore or elsewhere, in a bathing suit by the water, and me, with a kind of cape we'd made out of I don't know what material; I'm carrying a kind of little wooden stretcher and on the other side another guy is holding it, in the middle, on the board, there's a box no bigger than a shoebox, but I think it's made of wood, and on it there's that cross painted in black.

I stayed like that looking at the picture for a long time. Is that what death was? A box. Was that our game? Did we invent that? I recalled Father One Hundred, when we had that little ritual to celebrate the idea and the beginning of the countdown.

In one hundred days we leave.

In one hundred days we're going home, it's over, it was over, and the other pictures too, that slightly blurred picture of us in the open truck and under the hats and the sun and the sun-glasses there are laughs, one of the guys is holding up a slate, with something written on it in chalk, *Class of 1962*, another's wearing a sign saying "*Going Home!*" around his neck, hanging from a string; and I remember that my hands were shaking and why suddenly I needed to look at the photos faster and faster, as if I were short of breath, couldn't breathe, and I looked at all of them once, then twice, then I wanted to see some of them one more time, but nothing, still nothing. I was filled with a great emptiness, a sensation of great emptiness, a great hollow. And yet I was trying to remember. And yet there were smells of burning straw and screams in my ear, the smell of dust in my nose, and trails in front of me, frightened looks but where was that, which photos, none of them, the photos were too intent on removing me from everything, like the things we brought back, those gypsum flowers so ridiculous when I think back, but we kept them and they're here, somewhere, in the dining-room cabinet, next to the souvenirs from our vacations in Spain and the Balearic Islands.

And I remember the shame I felt when I came back from over there, when we had returned, one after the other, except for Bernard—at least he spared himself the humiliation of coming back here and doing what we did: keep quiet, show photos, yes, sun, beautiful landscapes, the sea, the traditional costumes, and vacation landscapes to keep a bit of sun in one's head, but the war, no, no war, there wasn't any war; and there's no use looking at those photos again and looking for at least one, just one that could have told me,

Yes, that's war, that's what war looks like, like the pictures you see on TV or in the papers, not like those summer camps, or those people filling the streets of Oran either, and the stores open, the city traffic, and then, how come on the walls I photographed I didn't find one single graffiti saying *Algeria will win*, not one wall painted, scraped, sandpapered, repainted, not one graffiti, not one weapon, nothing, nothing but that emptiness, and the sun, the blue sky, and the monstrosity of that beautiful weather.

The pictures of the sea.

All the guys on the deck smoking and looking at the horizon, hazy, distant—or on the contrary, in the night, the roaring of the engines and the wind, and how astonishing it is for a peasant to discover that a propeller can be out of the water, as if the ship were going to fly away and the crash it makes when it falls back, the ground so unstable and constantly shifting.

In some pictures there's just a blur in the distance, so you can't guess if it's arrival or departure. The only thing I remember is that the first time I saw the sea it was in Marseilles, the weather was cold and gray, and I was about to board a ship for Algeria.

MORNING

SOMETHING MADE ME JUMP AND I DIDN'T KNOW IF IT was because I'd been sleeping or if I'd just heard a noise in the hallway.

I straightened up and hurriedly grabbed the photographs, stuffing them into both hands without thinking, only focused on putting them back quickly into the envelopes, without sorting them, then throwing the envelopes into the shoebox. As if I didn't want Nicole to see me. As if I had to justify myself for being there and looking at those old pictures, and say what, say what again, so I got up and very quickly walked across the living room to put the shoebox back from where I'd taken it, in the hallway closet.

Nicole was standing there, in front of me.

I closed the closet door and saw her waiting and looking at me with her bathrobe open, and her eyes—she thought twice and didn't ask any questions, she closed her bathrobe, put a hand on the radiator, and I know she would have liked to ask me why I wasn't sleeping—and her eyes staring at me again to ask what I was doing there, embarrassed or upset as I must have seemed to her.

Maybe she would have liked to tell me what time it was, so early already, still so early,

Since when have you been up, come back to bed, go to sleep, you need to sleep, we're going to get up in an hour—but she didn't say anything.

She just asked if I wanted my coffee right away. I said I was going to make it and she could go back to bed. Because that was the thing, too, I wanted to be by myself, wait some more, maybe think, or even just hear the coffee in the coffeepot, first hear it flowing up and then listen to the sharp click of the switch turning off, and finally pour the coffee, smell its aroma, feel its warmth through the bowl and drink slowly, in little sips, cautiously, the way you take one step after another, and move toward the day like that, gently, gradually, and get hold of myself too, little by little.

I sat there alone drinking my coffee, in the kitchen. That's when I wondered what was going to happen, how I would manage to go all the way to the church square, or maybe before that to Solange's place, I wondered.

I couldn't see a thing, not one meter of future ahead of me.

I put on my old woolen coat, I took my boots, gloves, and I walked through the fields for close to an hour. I walked up the fields along the frozen furrows and I saw the sky rising in the distance, the night dissolving, slowly, petrol blue and pinkish filaments stretching out in the nearly white sky far off, the crows in the black trees. The first new houses. The telephone poles along the road. I saw all that and I tasted the cold, the white breath coming out of my mouth and nose and also the silence like a picture under cellophane, frozen and cold, but not sad—I wasn't sad, just worried about what to do later.

And also, I was saying to myself,

No, maybe I won't do anything, I'm going to wait at home and I won't do anything.

I wondered why I should be thinking of Bernard again, now. Only of him.

And I had to admit that what I hated in him wasn't him, nor what he had been when he was young, nor anything about him, but just seeing him every day, on the street, him, in life, dragging around our mutual history in his whole body, in his presence and even in his way of having become what he became. And what bothers me is that he became what I might have become too, if I'd been able not to accept certain things.

But now I can stay home, here, sit down and tell myself I have to drive away all those images, and answer yes when I hear Nicole,

You want some more coffee?

Yes.

Not think, pick up the bowl I had put in the sink. Then look at the water flowing out of the faucet into the bowl. Fill it up and let the water overflow and come out again spurting up like a fountain. And then clean the bowl, rinse it, wash my hands under the warm water and dry it before handing it to Nicole. I didn't look at her; she probably knew what I was thinking.

And yet, did I ever tell her things from over there? When I got back from over there did I take the time to say,

You know, Nicole, we cry in the night because one day we're branded for life by such horrific images that we can't bear to tell them to ourselves.

I sat down and drank the coffee with my eyes staring at my bowl so as not to see, just letting too much coffee turn my stomach, and I thought again of the ants that used to crawl over our hands when we were waiting with our rifles all day long, on duty outside, on the lookout for who knows what, a *mechta*, a cave, a thicket, the brush.

And then I remember how the insects used to drive us crazy, we saw them everywhere, in the walls, in our heads; we would scratch ourselves because of the dirt and the insects, but sometimes it was just grains of sand.

Sitting there with my coffee, I couldn't raise my head or even hear Nicole moving around, getting up, sitting down, it was painful to hear the sound of dishes, of a closet being opened or closed. I remember being startled at the slightest noise. From fatigue. I would say to myself,

It's because I'm tired. I didn't sleep, not enough, and that's why, not at all because of that square courtyard I always see again from above, from a loggia, just this one image in my mind, a square piece of yellow-white ground, and I tell myself how at first I loved that coolness when they put me there to guard the prisoners. And then—

The screams, the crying, the groans. The silences, too long.

And then—

And then I drove to the church and of course nobody was there yet, not in the square, not on the road.

I didn't pass anybody in the early morning hours, too early, the road still too gray, and when I stopped at the square I didn't dare turn off the engine. I stayed like that for how long, a good twenty minutes, and I listened to the news on the radio for a while—actually I didn't really listen, I let the voices fill the car along with the fan of the heater. I opened the window and leaned out, the icy air getting me. I heard the church bells. It was a quarter past seven, or half past, I didn't know, and I was saying to myself they'll be here soon, or maybe, no, not soon, in a while, in an hour or two.

I kept telling myself there was no use staying there, waiting.

I thought Patou would open soon, and, why not, I could go over there and have another cup of coffee. I thought that and yet without thinking I released the hand brake and slowly started the car. Although I could have got out and walked over to Patou's.

But no.

I cranked up the window again and drove off. I drove very slowly.

Without really knowing where I was going.

What I realized at that moment was that I had made up my mind not to go with the gendarmes to Bernard's place. And I wouldn't go for coffee either, or see Patou again to hear her tell me, so early in the morning,

Maybe he'll apologize and the Chefraouis won't press charges, maybe they,

Maybe none of that matters, that whole story doesn't matter, maybe you don't know what a real story is if you haven't lifted the ones underneath, the only ones that count, they're like ghosts, our ghosts, that accumulate and are like the stones of a strange house where you lock yourself in all alone, each one of us in his own house, and with what windows, how many windows? And at that moment, I thought we should move as little as possible during our lifetime so as not to generate the past, as we do, every day, the past that creates stones, and the stones, walls. And now we're here watching ourselves grow old, not understanding why Bernard is out there in that shack, with his dogs so old now, and his memory so old, and his hatred so old too that all the words we could say can't do very much.

I won't go to Patou's or Solange's house, nor go see anybody who could still be tempted to tell me, to explain, who would want to convince me.

I have nothing to learn. Nothing I want to know. Nothing I want to begin hearing again, or wait for, or relive—except that maybe I'd like to know why we take pictures and why they make us believe that we don't have a stomachache and that we sleep fine.

Algeria. Oran. 1961.

I can see myself again, I had looked at her handbag with its two lanyards hanging from the zipper, lying next to her on the table of the café where we'd arranged to meet. I was the one who'd given Bernard's address to Mireille, because she was really in distress and embarrassed, too, apologizing profusely to me, as if that fight could have been avoided and it was all her fault. I said no, you couldn't possibly know.

But if I'd been there.

If you had come, yes.

And she'd gone on like that, she was worried, she wanted to find Bernard and explain to him why she hadn't come that day—her father, the vines in his vineyard ripped up, her father, who had cursed the French Army, incapable of defending him. That's all. And cursed all the draftees too, de Gaulle's scheme to avoid a putsch. That's what her father had said. And the other girls hadn't come because of her, she had called them and they'd decided not to go out without her.

What she knew, on the other hand, was how as time went by she was beginning to see the world around her collapsing, and friendships too, friends who didn't talk to her anymore. She talked about Philibert, saying he was a traitor, I even remember she said it with such anger in her voice that it made it seem deeper, almost masculine; and she had put her glasses back on to disappear behind them and keep on railing about Philibert and his Spanish pals.

All communists, all agreeing with the terrorists, they're for the terrorists and independence, and now they say that because of people like my father all the French from here are going to be hated everywhere, by everybody, nobody will want us, we'll lose here, we'll be driven out, out of our home, and in France they'll look at us with scorn, disdain, and hatred, that's what Philibert says, he talks about History with a capital H and he claims we're wrong because we're from another time, selfish, blind, and when I said that to my father, he said I couldn't see him again. But I don't feel like seeing him again anyway. Not Philibert and not the Spaniards, none of them, she'd said.

I drove up toward La Migne, and went on further, toward La Croix des Femmes Mortes, and from there I looked down at the villages below, the snow, the frozen fields; then I drove faster. Without thinking. Without reflecting. It's just that I was remembering Mireille, how I saw her again a few times, and especially that time in the Choupot neighborhood in 1962. It wasn't really long before everything was all over, maybe in the bar where we had met the first time.

And that time she was alone again.

I saw her drink a cup of coffee; her face was livid, her hands were shaking, she was smoking nonstop. And she poured it all out, just like that, to me, the first guy to come along, a soldier she hardly knew anything about, someone she should even have snubbed and detested because it was my fault that she didn't see Bernard anymore. But no. She didn't hate me. She didn't like me either. She just needed to talk. Talk to someone who knew Bernard, maybe, and I was his cousin, the one who'd given her his address, and she told me—at first she didn't want to take off her glasses, and it's only because I insisted that she agreed just to raise them to, yes, to show me, so I could see,

He's going crazy, she said, papa's going crazy,

And ashamed, terribly pale, she had lowered her eyes over her cup to tell how her father had become enraged because he'd found Bernard's letters, and on reading them he understood everything, yes, what both of them wanted, to go to Paris, get married, work over there, have children. The father had yelled and slapped his daughter—no, not slapped, a slap doesn't do what I saw, and yet that's the word she used,

He slapped me.

And she hadn't screamed. She'd let herself get hit because she knew she couldn't answer when he yelled,

You won't leave, traitors leave and we kill traitors, that's all, and the army, a soldier, de Gaulle's lousy soldiers who let the others loot and destroy and kill, and our land, our homes, everything that's ours, he'd yelled, they won't get a thing and you, I forbid you to leave.

And she'd told me all this, that she hadn't screamed or budged when her father hit her. She managed to hold back her tears. She was proud, even at that moment, proud when she told me she'd endured his blows without flinching, because she respected her father.

And she was smiling. I will remember that, she was smiling.

And that smile, I also remember wondering if it wasn't the most disturbing thing in all of that, more than the purple marks around her eye, more than that suitcase next to her which she told me she had packed that very morning.

And on the road the thought came to me that not once did Bernard speak of her again, of how they'd lived together near Paris and also how, I remember, there was nothing really surprising about what happened to them, her hands too soft, not made for work. She absolutely didn't believe that French Algeria could come to an end. She was in her dream and she couldn't believe that she, too, would find herself having to leave just like the others, without having chosen to, with no hope of return.

And yet it happened. And not when I saw her, there, with her suitcase, but a few weeks later. And then, it wasn't the same at all, it was over, I suddenly remember that it was over, the Evian Accords signed so far away from us, from where we were, turning into shouts of joy, and the strident ululations of the women, the horns honking, everything was coming to us and Oran plunged into a madness impossible to relate, to describe; I remember how we were crisscrossing the city and suddenly the city wasn't the same anymore, all those people fearlessly—fearless at last—letting the joy they had in their hearts explode, with nothing holding them back anymore, a whole people standing up, mad with freedom, suddenly, as if, looking at them, we were facing what our parents had felt not even twenty years before, when the Germans left France, that happiness, that jubilation, the great joy a crowd is capable of when it gets carried away, I remember that, the wild, beautiful emotion of the Algerian people—

and that's when the car skidded.

Slightly. An ice patch, frost. I was driving a little too fast, too far to the right. The car skidded. I felt it skidding—but slowly, gently, I had the reflex of not using the brake and slowing down, letting the car skid.

And then it tipped over into a ditch.

It happened gently, without violence. The car skidded to the right, completely, the whole right side. The ditch wasn't very deep, but deep enough so there was no way I could get the car out of it by myself. So I opened the door and tried to get out of the car. I did not succeed. Or I gave up, I don't know anymore. The road would remain deserted for another hour or two perhaps, maybe more on a Sunday morning so early, I told myself it would be a long time before anybody drove by.

I closed the door and looked to my left at the little woods where the nearest treetops were covering part of the road with their shadow. On the other side, to the right, there were fields. Just a stretch of snow really, very far, very vast, all the way down to where there was a farmhouse. But it was very far. Not a sound. Or only that cawing in the trees, the sound of the wet branches grinding against each other.

And me, in the car.

I let the engine idle to have a little heat. Then I turned it off. And I remember, in front of me, the little tarred road that continued straight ahead, and nothing in front of me, nothing, nothing but those things surging up in me, that overflow, and the desire to—Mireille's hands, too fragile, Mireille who didn't have the faintest idea of what it would be like to make a living cleaning apartments or taking in sewing, not the faintest idea what it would be like to find herself there with Bernard, who would not have his garage, ever, but work at Renault on the assembly line like everybody else, in a factory, and the pace to keep, the schedules, the metro, a life she had no idea of, in which neither youth, nor her favorite pop stars, nor the banks of the Seine would ever be more than an aborted dream she would mourn for from time to time, on Sunday mornings perhaps, as she would probably tell her parents in long, apologetic letters full of regrets which her father would never open.

And she would resent Bernard, she'd make him the guilty party, since there has to be one.

I suspected it from the start, as soon as I had seen how she expected everything from him, and too much from everything, how she didn't realize that life would never again be easy for her, just as she didn't understand when she saw her father take up arms that day and stand at his window to fire at the first men to approach, she saw that, she saw a world shudder and fall when she thought it was eternal and strong. She saw it sink in the springtime, she saw men, several of them together pushing cars, their Dauphine, their Aronde, neighbors helping to push the car it took them years to pay for, and the car falling over the parapet with a metallic crash, like candy wrappers you crumple up and throw away, and they'll leave nothing behind, they'll leave nothing for anybody, that was on every face, we won't leave them a thing, and she saw women and little girls and boys crying and thinking they would die here, abandoned, alone, and around them there were men, neighbors, uncles, they were the men and they didn't want to leave anything behind, they chopped apart the furniture with axes, the old family furniture was thrown out the windows, and from the apartments came the smell of fire, furniture was burning in the courtyards, in the gardens, dishes were smashed, everything, nothing will remain but ravaged, frightened faces on the side of the roads, on the docks, at the airport, and suddenly whole streets with little trucks loaded to the vomiting point, men with a cigarette between their lips standing on the running boards to keep chairs and tables from falling, employees, faces you've seen every day for years, and now they were about to leave and disappear and tell themselves they'd never come back here and in France they would see them coming, the colonists, the ones in a hurry to sell some wretched object before they left, businesses they were abandoning with rage in their guts and a heavy heart, their whole life and their ancestors' remains rotting in cemeteries they'd never see again and the weeds would ravage them—and still that jubilation I remember it and the isolated snipers too, up there in the buildings, or above them, guys firing, who thought they could turn everybody against them and still go on that way when it was all over, and at the end the firing was coming from the wealthy neighborhoods, shots you could hardly hear over the ululations of the women, and the women and children in the streets, and the flags suddenly hoisted up as if out of nowhere, the Algerian flag that Mireille didn't even know existed, she saw it at a moment when she found herself all alone in the street, I know it, I saw her afterward, on the dock, she was on the dock and we were there looking at the ships and the people who had to be directed, helped, people who were crying, people who were walking straight ahead, without turning around, people who got into fights over everything and anything, and we soldiers had to separate them because one had just shoved the other a little and they were ready to kill each other on the spot, the women with children in their arms, the children with dolls in their arms, and the dolls with their empty eyes, blue as the blue of the livid sky, and luckily the sea was gentle, the ships were leaving and you could see a whiff of foam in their wake, and necks obstinately determined not to turn around for a last look at what they were leaving behind, let's look straight ahead, at what we'll become, at everything we will become, that's how they could bear it, without understanding, carrying their suitcases and others putting off the moment, others laughing, I saw some of them laughing and waving wildly, smoking, clowning around like schoolboys to drive off the fear of tomorrow, and also, something that—this must be said, admitted, the faces of the others, the ones you'd rather not talk about, like that lieutenant I saw burst into tears because he couldn't answer them, he couldn't tell them they would be left behind, abandoned, they wouldn't have believed it, not one of them would have believed it, they'd been promised, the army, France, everybody had promised and nobody kept his promise and I remember, and others remember, and all of us remember how the *harkis* were forced to get back down from the trucks that were leaving, and also the rifle butts hitting them so they wouldn't climb back into the trucks, their screams, the stupor, the disbelief on their faces, they couldn't believe it, we didn't believe it either but we were doing it, the rifle butts hitting their hands so they wouldn't get on, and we left them to yell, howl, and cry, we left them, abandoned them and betrayed them, we knew what would happen, what would happen to them, by the thousands, and Idir like the others, Idir among the others, his face fading now into the death of the others, of all the others, I know it well because I saw that, I saw it, I also saw how hundreds of them were forced to drink gasoline and how they were set on fire and the bodies burnt like that—Idir died and all I did was watch, wondering what I was seeing and if I was seeing and hearing men we betrayed, and the Algerian flag and the women's ululations and the crazies from the OAS going through the streets to gun down all the Europeans who wanted to leave, and on the walls OAS, everywhere the OAS, their bombs still going off, to the bitter end, the windows shattering, bodies falling in the night, and dogs crossing the sidewalks for a piece of meat in a garbage can, the garbage can falling over and us, still there for a few weeks more, waiting for it all to be over, waiting to go home, leave Algeria, and say it's over—

and.

I stayed in the car like that. And then all of a sudden I was glad the car was stuck in the snow, glad I couldn't move anymore, at all. I thought I just had to wait, it felt good, too, for a while, that nothing moved, it felt good to stay put, as if I were hanging by a thread. At some point I listened to the radio a little, then nothing but the silence. I thought again of Bernard, of Chefraoui. I thought of Solange again, who was probably with the gendarmes.

I told myself for the first time that I felt like going back there, maybe, and that I'd like to see if there are farmhouses with square courtyards, almost white, and if there are children playing soccer in their bare feet. I would like to see if Algeria exists and if I, too, had left something more than my youth back there. I'd like to see, I don't know. I'd like to see if the air is as blue as in my memories. If they still eat *kémias*. I'd like to see something that doesn't exist but lives inside yourself, something you keep like a dream, a resonant, palpitating world, I would like to, I don't know, I never knew what I wanted, there, in the car, just not hear the bombardments or the screams anymore, not know what a charred body smells like anymore, or the smell of death—I'd like to know if you can begin to live when you know it's already too late.

GLOSSARY

bled French word for village, from the Arabic.

bicot Racist, insulting French slang term for Arab.

caoua French slang word for coffee, from the Arabic.

djebel Arabic word for a mountainous area.

Evian Accords Agreement signed March 18, 1962, in Évian-les-Bains, France, by representatives of the provisional government of Algeria and the French government, ending the Algerian War. France recognized Algeria as an independent state.

fellagha From the Arabic: fighter for Algerian independence; shortened by the French to "fell" (plural of the Arabic fellagh, "one who cuts off roads").

gendarmes	Members of a national police force in France under the jurisdiction of the army. They serve as the police in rural areas and on highways, much like state troopers in the United States.
harkis	Algerian Arabs who fought with the French Army against the Algerians in their war for independence.
Kabyle	Someone from Kabylia, a mountainous region in Algeria.
kémias	North African hors d'oeuvres.
méchoui	A large, festive lamb roast in which a whole sheep is barbecued. From the Arabic.
mechta	Arabic word for small village.
OAS	Abbreviation for Organisation de l'Armée Secrète, an illegal, far-right nationalist movement violently opposed to Algerian independence that carried out acts of terror in both Algeria and France in the 1960s.
Oradour-sur-Glane	Town in France where, in June 1944, German SS troops massacred the entire population: 642 men, women, and children.
Verdun	Town in northern France, and the site of the bloodiest battle of World War I, ending in a French victory in 1917. The battle resulted in more than 360,000 French and 335,000 German casualties.
wadi	From the Arabic: a ravine made by a dried-out riverbed.